***Brin came to an abrupt standstill
at the door.***

Riley was stretched out on the bed, his head propped up on the headboard. "Everybody gone?"

"What are you doing here?"

"Resting. Do you realize I was on my feet for almost four hours straight?"

"You know what I mean," she cried angrily. "What are you doing here? In my bedroom. On my bed. I thought you'd gone home."

"Home?" he asked. "I don't have a *home*. I have a *house* that used to be a home . . . when I shared it with my wife."

She turned away from him, kicking off her shoes. Facing the mirror, she ran her hands through her hair. "I'm tired."

"You look it. Come lie down." He patted the space beside him on the bed. In the mirror he looked as tempting as the apple must have looked to Eve, and just as dangerous. . . .

## WHAT ARE *LOVESWEPT* ROMANCES?

They are stories of true romance and touching emotion. We believe those two very important ingredients are constants in our highly sensual and very believable stories in the *LOVESWEPT* line. Our goal is to give you, the reader, stories of consistently high quality that may sometimes make you laugh, sometimes make you cry, but are always fresh and creative and contain many delightful surprises within their pages.

Most romance fans read an enormous number of books. Those they truly love, they keep. Others may be traded with friends and soon forgotten. We hope that each *LOVESWEPT* romance will be a treasure—a "keeper." We will always try to publish

*LOVE STORIES YOU'LL NEVER FORGET*
*BY AUTHORS YOU'LL ALWAYS REMEMBER*

The Editors

LOVESWEPT® • 115

# Sandra Brown
# Riley in the Morning

BANTAM BOOKS
TORONTO • NEW YORK • LONDON • SYDNEY • AUCKLAND

RILEY IN THE MORNING

*A Bantam Book / November 1985*

*LOVESWEPT® and the wave device are registered
trademarks of Bantam Books, Inc. Registered in U.S. Patent
and Trademark Office and elsewhere.*

ISBN 0-553-21730-5

*Published simultaneously in the United States and Canada*

---

*Bantam Books are published by Bantam Books, Inc. Its
trademark, consisting of the words "Bantam Books" and
the portrayal of a rooster, is Registered in U.S. Patent and
Trademark Office and in other countries. Marca Registrada.
Bantam Books, Inc., 666 Fifth Avenue, New York, New
York 10103.*

---

PRINTED IN THE UNITED STATES OF AMERICA

O    0  9  8  7  6  5  4  3  2  1

# One

"Ms. Cassidy, dear?"

"Yes?"

"So sorry, darling, but your table simply isn't large enough."

"Damn," Brin muttered under her breath as she struggled with the zipper at the back of her dress. She twisted around to check in the mirror what was causing it to stick. When she turned, an electric curler slid out of her hair, leaving a heavy strand to fall over her eye. She shoved it off her face, looping it around one of the hair-curler pins that radiated from her head like a space-age halo. "Arrange everything as best you can, Stewart. Has the bartender arrived yet?"

"I *have* arranged everything as best I can," he said petulantly. "You need a larger table."

Brin's arms fell heavily to her sides. Glancing at

the harried image in the mirror, one eye artfully made up, the other as yet untouched, she called herself a fool for hostessing this party in the first place. She had timed everything down to the second. She didn't need any kinks in the tight schedule, such as a stuck zipper and a querulous caterer.

Turning, she flung open the bathroom door and confronted Stewart, who stood with his pale hands on his hips, wearing an expression just as sour as hers.

"I don't have a larger table," Brin said irritably. "Let's see what we can do. Is the bartender here yet?" On stocking feet she hurried through the bedroom, down the stairs, and into the dining room, where a buffet was being set up. Her dress was slipping off her shoulders, but then, there was no need to be too concerned about modesty in front of Stewart.

Two of his assistants were standing by, arms crossed idly over their chests, as though waiting for a bus. She shot them exasperated looks that didn't faze them in the slightest.

"Jackie said he'd be here by now," Stewart said of the missing bartender. "I can't imagine what's keeping him. We're *extremely* close."

"Why doesn't that make me feel better?"

Brin spoke the question under her breath as she studied the table. The food on the silver trays was attractively arranged and lavishly garnished, but the trays were jammed together, overlapping in places. Some extended over the edges of the table. Stewart might be difficult and aggravating, but he knew his stuff, and she couldn't argue with him. "You're right, we'll have to do some rearranging."

"It's that ghastly centerpiece," Stewart said, pointing with distaste. "You should have let me select the flowers. Remember I told you—"

"I remember, I remember, but I wanted to choose my own florist."

"Can't we remove the thing? Or at least let me rearrange it so it isn't so . . . so . . ." He made a descriptive gesture with his hands.

"You're not to touch it. I paid a hundred dollars for it."

"You get what you pay for," he said snidely.

She faced him angrily, hooking the errant strand of hair around another pin when it slipped from the first. "This has nothing to do with money. The florist happens to be a friend of mine, and she's been in the business longer than you've been alive."

I must be agitated, Brin thought. *Why am I standing here arguing with smug Stewart, when I'm only half dressed and forty guests are due to arrive at any moment?*

She returned her attention to the crowded table. "Can you leave some of the trays in the kitchen and replace the ones on the table as they empty?"

Stewart's hand fluttered to his chest and his mouth fell open in horror. "Absolutely not! My darling, these dishes are planned to alternately soothe and excite the palate. They're a blend of tart and—"

"Oh, for heaven's sake!" Brin cried. "Who will know in what order their palates are supposed to be soothed or excited? These people will just want to eat. I doubt they'll pay attention to anything except whether the food tastes good or not."

Gnawing her cheek in concentration, she scanned the table again. "All right," she said, her mind made up, "set that bowl of marinated shrimp on the coffee table in the living room. Have a cup of toothpicks nearby. And you," she said, pointing to one of the indolent assistants, "move that cheese tray over there by the bar. I think there's room for that chafing dish of Swedish meatballs on the table by the sofa. That should make room on the table."

The three young men rolled their eyes at one another. "You're a gastronomical philistine of the worst sort," Stewart said snippishly.

"Just do it. And where's that bartender you promised me? Nothing's set up."

"He'll be here."

"Well, he'd better be here soon, or I'm going to start deducting from your bill."

The doorbell chimed. "See?" Stewart said loftily. "No cause for panic. That's him now." He swished toward the front door before Brin had a chance to.

"Who are *you?*" The disembodied voice asking the rude question was deep and demanding.

Brin recognized the voice immediately and felt the earth drop out from under her.

"Oh my dear, I'm positively dying!" Stewart cried theatrically, his hands aflutter. "I can't believe it. She didn't tell me *you* would be among the party guests."

"What the hell are you talking about? What party?" the voice asked in a surly growl. "Where's Brin?"

She forced herself into motion and went toward the door, stepping in the line of vision of the man standing on the threshold. "Thank you, Stewart," she said quietly. "I believe you have work to do."

She was amazed at how calm she sounded. On

the inside, chaos reigned: Her vital organs were doing backward somersaults; her knees had turned the consistency of Stewart's famous tomato aspic; all the blood had drained from her head. But outwardly she presented a facade of aloofness that should have won her an Oscar at least.

After Stewart had moved out of earshot, she looked at the man. "What are you doing here, Riley?"

"Just thought I'd drop by." He propped his shoulder against the doorjamb and let his eyes— *damn those blue eyes*—drift over her. He seemed amused by the curlers in her hair, the unfastened dress she was having a hard time keeping up, and her stockinged feet.

"Well, you should have called before you came, because you couldn't have picked a more inconvenient time. You'll have to excuse me. I have guests due to arrive in a few minutes. I haven't finished my makeup—"

"That's not a kinky new fad? Making up just one eye?"

"—or touched my hair," she finished, ignoring his teasing. "The bartender hasn't shown up yet. And the caterer is being a colossal pain."

"Sounds like you need help." He shoved his way inside before Brin could stammer a protest. "You guys have everything under control?" he asked the three caterers, who were staring at him in awe.

"Everything's perfect, absolutely perfect, Mr. Riley," Stewart gushed. "Can we get you anything?"

"Riley," Brin ground out between her teeth.

"Hmm?" He turned around, supremely unconcerned about her apparent agitation.

"May I see you alone? Please."

"What, now?"

"Now."

"Sure, honey. The bedroom?"

"The kitchen." She walked stiffly past the three gaping caterers, saying, "Carry on," in as firm a voice as she could muster.

Angrily she pushed open the swinging door and stepped into the kitchen. She usually liked this room, with its classic black-and-white-checked tile floor, its spacious counter tops, and well-arranged appliances. Tonight it was cluttered with party paraphernalia, but she didn't notice any of it as she pivoted to face the man who was barely two steps behind her.

"Riley, what are you doing here?" She repeated the question with undisguised asperity.

"I wanted to see you."

"After seven months?"

"Has it been only seven months?"

"And you chose tonight by chance?"

"How was I supposed to know you were giving a party?"

"You could have called."

"It was a spur-of-the-moment decision."

"Isn't everything you do?" He frowned, and she drew a deep breath. No sense in getting unpleasant. "How did you know where I was living?"

"I knew." His eyes slowly took in the kitchen and the twilit view beyond the wide windows. "A Russian Hill address. I'm impressed."

"Don't be. I'm house sitting. A friend of mine went to Europe for two years."

"Anybody I know?"

"No, I don't think so. She's an old school chum."

Brin guarded against looking at him. When she looked at him, her eyes got greedy and wanted to take in every detail. She wouldn't punish herself that way.

"Lucky you. The day you walk out on me, your friend takes off for Europe. You couldn't have planned it better. Or did you plan it?"

Her eyes flew up to his. "Don't start this now, Riley."

"Don't you think seven months is long enough to stew about it? I want to know why my wife just checked out one day while I was at work."

Uneasy, she shifted from one foot to the other. "It wasn't like that."

"Then what was it like? Tell me. I want to know."

"Do you?"

"Yes."

"Well, you've taken your sweet time to find out. The reasons behind my leaving couldn't have been very important to you. Why did you get curious tonight, after seven months? Did one of your public appearances get canceled? Did you find yourself alone and without anything spontaneous or interesting to do?"

"Whew! Hitting below the belt, are we?" He socked her lightly in the tummy. Actually a little below the tummy. And well below the belt.

She jumped back in alarm at the effect even that touch had on her. "Will you please leave, Riley? I have guests coming. I've got to comb out my hair. I . . ."

Her voice faltered when he reached up and tugged sharply on the loose strand. He was smiling. "It's cute when it's all tumbled. Reminds me of what you look like when you first get out of bed."

"I . . . I haven't even finished dressing."

His eyes slid hotly down her body, all the way to her feet. "Your toes are so sweet."

"Riley."

"And sexy. Remember when we discovered each other's toes and what a turn-on dallying with them can be?"

"Riley!" Her fists were digging into her hips as she glared up at him. She was becoming more vexed by the moment. Vexed and aroused.

"In the hot tub, wasn't it?"

"Oh! There's just no talking to you." She spun on her heel and headed for the door. "I'm going upstairs. When I come down I expect you to be gone."

"Wait a minute." He caught her arm and drew her up short. "Your zipper's not done up all the way. No wonder that dress keeps falling off your shoulders. Not that I'm complaining. I could make a meal out of your shoulders. Are you trying to entice me with those brief glimpses of forbidden flesh?"

"Riley—"

"Hold still." His hands were at her waist. His knuckles brushed the skin of her back as he struggled to work the cloth from beneath the bite of the zipper without tearing it. "You almost mangled it."

"I was in a state even before you showed up."

"Over a zipper?"

"That was only the tip of the iceberg."

"Troubles?"

"Not 'troubles,' exactly. I just wanted everything to be nice tonight."

"So you really are having a party."

"Of course. What did you think?"

"I don't know. Maybe that you were taking up with Stewart's sort."

"Very funny. Aren't you done yet?"

With every heartbeat it was becoming more difficult to stand still. The touch of his hands was so achingly familiar. The scent of his breath as it fanned her neck was memory-stirring, and this husbandly chore of zipping her dress reminded her of other times, happy times she had tried to forget.

"Who's the party for?"

"The people I work with."

"At the radio station?"

So he knew where she was working now. Well, that hadn't taken any great detective work on his part. It had been published in all the local newspapers. In fact there had been quite a splash in media circles when Brin Cassidy left Jon Riley and his popular morning television talk show, *Riley in the Morning*, to accept a job producing a radio phone-in discussion program.

At the time there had been speculation on the future of their marriage, too. Living down the gossip columns, the published innuendos, the myriad invasions of privacy, had been hard to do. But that hadn't been the hardest thing. The hardest thing had been learning to live without Riley.

And now he was here, near, touching her again, and it took every ounce of self-discipline she had not to turn in his arms and hold him against her.

"Hurry, please, Riley."

"You still haven't told me what the occasion is."

"Mr. Winn's birthday."

"Ah-ha. That explains the cake." He nodded toward the tiered chocolate confection on the counter top.

"Haven't you fixed that zipper yet?"

"So Abel Winn himself will be here. President and CEO of the Winn Company."

"Do you know him?"

"I've met him once or twice." He finally succeeded in wresting the fabric free of the zipper and pulled it up. He fastened the hook and eye, which was a mere six inches above her waist, and bent his knees to reduce his height. He pecked a soft kiss directly between her bare shoulder blades, as had been his habit when they had shared a house, a bed, their bodies.

Brin gasped softly.

Stewart sailed through the door in time to see Brin's cheeks turning pink and Riley's grin widening as he rose to his full height again. "Well," the caterer drawled, "I take it you two know each other."

"He's . . . uh . . . he's my . . . uh . . ."

"Husband," Riley calmly supplied. "Can we help you with something?"

"Husband?" Stewart squeaked.

"Husband," Riley repeated, unruffled.

"Weeeell." Stewart gave Brin a once-over that was catty and covetous at the same time.

"What was it you wanted?" Riley asked.

His brisk tone snapped the caterer to attention. "I just came to tell Mrs. Riley that—"

"Ms. Cassidy," Brin corrected.

"Oh, certainly, Ms. *Cassidy.* I'm Stewart, by the way," he said to Riley with an ingratiating smile.

"Stewart." Riley nodded.

"A pleasure. Yes, well, Steve and Bart have done a simply *marvelous* job rearranging the trays. They'll be circulating all night to make sure they're replenished. I pinched a few of the most offensive buds—only a few, dear—from that centerpiece. It all looks quite smashing now."

"Fine," Brin said tightly, wishing with all her mind that Riley would lift his hands off her shoulders and put space between the front of his thighs and the backs of hers. Unfortunately her heart wanted no part of that wish.

"It might get a bit crowded when I flambé the Bananas Foster. I hope we don't set anyone on fire."

She could feel Riley's silent chuckle vibrating through his body. "I'm sure I can trust you to be careful."

"One teeny-weeny, tiny problem," Stewart added.

"What?"

"Jackie hasn't arrived yet. I can't imagine what got into him."

"Damned if I'd hazard a guess," Riley said for her ears alone.

She clamped down on her lower lip to keep from laughing out loud. A few minutes ago the absence of the bartender had sent her into a tailspin. Now that seemed a mild crisis, too insignificant to worry about. What she had to cope with now was the thrill that zinged through her every time she felt the front of Riley's trousers brush against her buttocks. "We'll make do, Stewart."

"The boys wanted me to ask, is *he* staying?" He pointed to Riley.

"Yes." "No." They answered in unison, Riley in the affirmative, Brin in the negative.

"Oh, I just adore sticky little situations like this," Stewart cooed.

"This isn't a sticky little situation. Will you please excuse us? We'll give you back the kitchen in just a moment," Brin said by way of dismissal.

"Of course." He left, after winking at her and blowing Riley a kiss.

Brin did an about-face with military precision. "You can't stay, Riley. I'm asking you to leave."

"You need me." She wondered if that statement carried a double meaning but decided it didn't when he added, "To tend bar."

"One of Stewart's assistants can do that."

"You heard him. Steve and Bart will be circulating all night."

"Then I'll handle it."

"The hostess? Don't be ridiculous. And Stewart is out because he'll be handling the food and pinching offensive buds. But if he tries to flambé *my* banana, I'll punch him out."

She gritted her teeth to keep from laughing. Dammit, she didn't want Riley to be funny and charming. She sure didn't want him to smile that slow, sexy smile or look at her with those eyes that were so achingly, beautifully blue.

"Face it, Brin. You haven't got a choice. Now, get your adorable tush upstairs and finish dressing. Brush out your hair. Give the lashes on your left eye a lick of the mascara wand and let me take over down here. Oh, and don't forget your shoes."

Her father had always said that a good soldier knew when to surrender with dignity. Brin recognized defeat and gave in to it graciously. "You can start getting things ready, but if Jackie shows up, I'll expect you to leave without causing a scene."

"What do I do first?" Riley shrugged off his jacket and tossed it across a chair at the kitchen table.

He was wearing a sports shirt and jeans under the poplin windbreaker. Expensive, true. Tasteful, true. The height of fashion, true. But she didn't want him to look so devastatingly gorgeous when he had seen her, for the first time in seven months, looking like the survivor of a shipwreck. "You're not even dressed for a party," she grumbled.

"California chic."

"But this is a semiformal affair."

"So I'll be an oddity." He had raised his voice, slightly but discernibly. Yet it was all honey and velvet when he added, "Besides, I could name times when you preferred me without any clothes at all." His eyes penetrated hers. "*Numerous* times."

She wet her lips. In this skirmish, he was the victor, unconditionally. "Lemons and limes are there," she said, pointing to the counter top, where the fruit was still wrapped in plastic bags. "Slice them. Drain those jars of olives, cocktail onions, and cherries. Put them in those shallow dishes. The bar's adjacent to the dining room."

"I'll find it. Glasses?"

"Dozens of them. At the bar."

"Ice?"

"Two full chests under the bar."

"Set ups?"

"They're there too."

"Piece of cake," he said arrogantly. "Where's a knife?"

"Second drawer to the right of the sink."

He found one and wielded it with the flourish of a fencer. "Scat."

Before she could lunge across the kitchen and kiss him just for being so damn cute, she did exactly as he suggested. Upstairs at the marble dressing table in the bathroom, she fumbled with the eye crayons, eye-shadow wands, shading blushers, and lipstick brushes. It was a wonder she didn't end up looking like a clown-school dropout. Miraculously, the results both highlighted her best features and appeared beautifully natural.

As she was stepping into her shoes, she heard the doorbell chime. She hoped Stewart would act as temporary host while she put in her earrings, misted herself with fragrance, added a final pat to her hair, and slid a thin diamond bracelet on her wrist. She leaned down to smooth her stocking. The bracelet caught on the sheer nylon and put a run in it.

With a barrage of unladylike cursing, she rummaged in her hosiery drawer, hoping that this wasn't her last pair of near-black stockings. It wasn't, but by the time she had put on the new pair, she was in a tizzy. The doorbell continued to ring with maddening frequency.

And the hostess hadn't yet put in an appearance!

It was Riley's fault, she thought as she rushed down the stairs. How dare he sabotage her party? How dare he ruin tonight for her?

Riley, Riley, Riley.

Why had he selected tonight to seek her out? He had had seven months to contact her, seven months in which she hadn't received so much as a telephone call from him. But doing things in an ordinary, mannerly fashion wasn't Riley's style. No, no, he had picked tonight to come see her, the worst possible night for him to show up on her doorstep.

He's looking well. *Who are you kidding, Brin? He looks positively wonderful.*

Perhaps a trifle thinner. *Your imagination. God knows there are plenty of women willing to cook for him if he asked them to.*

Didn't you notice more gray hair? *It only makes his eyes look bluer.*

No matter how good he looks, or how charming he acts, he has no right to crash your party. And no matter how shaky you are, you are *not* glad to see him. *And the Golden Gate Bridge isn't in San Francisco.*

Taking a deep breath, she stepped off the bottom stair and into the friendly confusion of the party.

"Brin, we were beginning to think you'd skipped out on your own party."

"You look beautiful."

"Great dress. Why haven't you ever worn it to work?"

"Because we wouldn't have gotten any work done, you bozo."

Brin was surrounded by the guests who had already arrived. She exchanged pleasantries with them, apologizing profusely for being late coming downstairs. "Help yourselves to the buffet and bar."

"We already have. And don't think we didn't notice the celebrity guest."

Past their shoulders Brin spied Riley at the bar. He was handling highballs and wine bottles as adroitly as a juggler. A ring of adoring females had formed around him. She was suddenly glad she had told her new colleagues that her separation from Riley was an amicable one. With any luck, no one would find his presence here tonight odd.

"Riley put in a surprise appearance," she said distantly, watching as Riley playfully ate a cherry proffered by one of his admirers. The woman giggled as his teeth closed around it and lifted it from her fingers.

"You mean he wasn't invited?"

Brin didn't like being backed into a corner, and recognized a loaded question when she heard one. Shaking herself out of her trance, she beamed a nonchalant smile and said, "Please excuse me. The caterer is still at the door welcoming my guests."

She shouldered her way through the thickening crowd, joking and smiling welcome as she went. "Thank you, Stewart," she said as she relieved him at the door. "You've gone above and beyond the call of duty."

"It'll be reflected on my bill. I've got popovers in the oven. They could have burned, you know."

Before the evening was out, she was going to smack him. It seemed destined to happen.

"Hello, so glad you could come. Let me take your coats." She turned on the charm as group after group of guests filled up the house. When she opened the door to Abel Winn, her plastic smile gave way to one of heartfelt warmth. "Our guest of honor. Happy birthday, Abel."

He was a man of indeterminate age, immaculately groomed, compactly and sturdily built. He wasn't very tall, but he exuded self-assurance and had the bearing of a born leader. His eyes reflected an intelligence that bordered on shrewdness. His smile for Brin was genuine, and softened the features of an otherwise stern, Teutonic face.

"Brin, dear, you shouldn't have done all this on my behalf." He leaned forward as he clasped her hand between both of his. "But I'm glad you did. I love parties. Especially when they're in my honor."

She laughed with him and ushered him inside. "There's food and drink aplenty. Help yourself."

"Won't you join me?"

"I still have hostess duties to carry out. Maybe later."

"I'll look forward to the time." He drew a more serious expression. "And speaking of time . . ."

"It's running out. I know. Tomorrow is the deadline you gave me."

"Have you made a decision?"

"Not yet, Abel."

"I was hoping your acceptance would be my birthday present tonight."

"It's a big decision." Inadvertently her eyes sought out Riley. She was disconcerted when she met his blue gaze from across the room. There was a crease of disapproval between his dark brows as he stared at her and Abel. "Please give me until tomorrow. I promise to give you my answer then."

"I'm certain it will be the one I want to hear. We'll talk later." Abel patted her hand before releasing it and moving into the midst of the party.

Someone had turned on the stereo. Conversation had risen above the level of the blaring music. The party was in full swing. It might have had an inauspicious beginning, but Brin was gratified to see that it was going well.

"It's all wonderful, Brin. You've outdone yourself." The woman who sidled up to her was dressed in jade satin. Brin recognized her as a member of the sales department at the radio station.

"Thank you."

"How did you ever manage?"

"Don't ask," Brin returned with a grimace. "Right up to the last minute it was disaster with a capital *d*."

"Well, it all came together beautifully. Your idea to have Jon Riley act as bartender was inspired. You must have a *very* friendly separation. How'd you ever talk him into it?"

"Just lucky, I guess."

The woman was so busy gobbling up Riley with her eyes that she failed to catch Brin's sarcasm. Objectively, Brin tried to view him through the other woman's eyes. He was heart-stoppingly handsome. Salt-and-pepper hair, cut and arranged to look as rakish as possible. Yet boyish, with a few strands carelessly falling over his forehead. An open invitation for a woman to run her fingers through it.

His face was lean and angular, the bone structure lending itself to a television camera's most discerning angle. A strong jaw. Slender nose, slightly flared over the straight, narrow lips. Lips that had dimples in each corner as strategically placed as punctuation marks.

His eyes were a color of blue the heavens would envy. "When you look at me, it's like being raped by an angel," she had told him once during a romantic interlude. He had thought she was just flattering him. He hadn't understood, but another woman would have. When he looked at a woman in that special, private way, his eyes pierced straight through her. It was violation, but the sweetest, dearest penetration imaginable.

His physique was tall, almost lanky, but hard and muscular. He could drape a shapeless burlap sack over that rangy body and make it look like high fashion. Clothes had been invented for bodies like his. He looked good without clothes too. Six feet four inches of tanned skin. Shadowed by soft, dark body hair. Chest hair that would make a woman's mouth water.

And he knew it.

As Brin and her companion continued to watch, Stewart went behind the bar and said something to Riley, embellishing it with wild gestures. Riley said something back, something that was obviously not to Stewart's liking. The caterer put his hands on his hips and screwed his face up into a comical pucker. Riley's gaze searched the room until it landed on Brin. Since his hands were busy, he jerked his chin up, indicating that she was needed.

"Excuse me." She wended her way through the crowd to the bar. "What is it?"

"Ask him," Riley said tersely.

"Well?" She looked at Stewart.

"Some *person*," Stewart said, "a terribly crude bruiser from Oklahoma or someplace equally as barbaric, is drinking *beer*, of all the ungodly things."

"The point, Stewart, the point," Brin said.

"He asked for salted nuts. Nuts! I mean, really! And I asked *him*"—he emphasized, pointing limply at Riley—"if he had any nuts and—"

"And I told him to stay the hell away from me."

Oh, Lord. She was getting a killer of a headache,

and it hurt all the way down to her toenails. "I think I have a can of nuts in the kitchen. I'll get it."

The kitchen was almost as quiet and serene as a church, in contrast to the racket and chaos beyond its door. Brin went into the butler's pantry and switched on the light. She moved aside boxes of cereal and crackers, searching for the can of cashews she remembered seeing there several days ago. A shadow fell across her. "Just a minute, Stewart, and I'll find them. I know they're in here somewhere."

"I'm sure Stewart will be glad to hear that."

"Riley!" she exclaimed, spinning around at the sound of that honey-coated voice, which was a sound technician's dream. "Where's Stewart?"

"I left him mixing a Scotch and water. I think he can handle that."

Her eyes rounded with surprise when he reached for the doorknob and closed them into the closet. It was actually a roomy pantry, but with two people closed inside it, the dimensions seemed to shrink. "What are you doing?"

"Locking you in."

"But—"

"I've missed you, Brin."

"This is—"

"And I don't intend to wait another second for a taste of you."

# Two

His mouth, from the instant it touched hers, was hungry and demanding. There was no preliminary investigation, no subtle teasing, no testing the waters, no time for her to protest or prepare herself for the onslaught. In a heartbeat his lips were on hers. Hotly possessive. Provocative. Persuasive.

Brin's rational self took a giant step backward, separating itself from her and leaving her defenseless and responsive. The taste, the texture, the heat of the kiss were all so familiar. She sank into it as one snuggles into an old, comfortable robe.

No other man could kiss like Riley. Oh, she remembered that thrusting pressure of his tongue. Yes, yes, just like that. Deep and swirling and greedy, as though he'd die for want of her. And that feathering caress against the roof of her mouth. The withdrawal, slow and sensuous. A leisurely sweep against her teeth. A damp licking of her lips.

"I've missed you. So much. I couldn't stand it another day. I had to see you. Brin, Brin . . ."

He kissed her again, and she heard wanton sounds emanating from her own throat. Her body responded in that warm, fluid way that inevitably leads to making love.

He was hard.

Yes, she remembered that too. His virility.

And now she felt it against the velvet-clad softness of her belly. If she didn't stop this now, things would get out of hand and she would hate herself later. Her body's yearning was powerful, but she fought it.

"Riley, no." The command didn't carry much weight, since it was issued on a breathy sigh. Brin was amazed that she could speak at all. His lips were moving softly over her neck, taking love bites. His tongue dipped into the triangle at the base of her throat. "Ahh, Riley, no, please."

"You still like that, do you?"

"No."

"Liar."

And her whimper proved him right. His hand moved down to her breast and she trembled against him. "Stop, Riley."

"Stop what? This?"

His agile thumb did some of its best work. She groaned. "I mean it. Stop. This is crazy."

"This is beautiful." He buried his face in her neck even as his caress brought about the response he craved. "So beautiful."

Another kiss followed, less urgent than the first,

but a thousand times more evocative. She went limp against him. "This is so unfair."

"Damn right. I want you naked."

"No, I mean . . . hmm . . . I could kill you for this."

His laugh was little more than a silent gust of breath in her ear. "How can you blame me? You look delectable. I always liked you in black."

The black velvet creation was a rare find, and Brin had known it the moment she saw the dress on a sale rack in Magnin's. It had long dolman sleeves that tapered to her wrist. The skirt was narrow and fit her hips to perfection. It was banded just below her knees with black satin. The neckline was high and cut straight across from the point of one shoulder to the other. Virtually backless, the dress was scooped out to mere inches above her waist.

She wished now that there were something between her skin and Riley's fingers as they lightly strummed her spine. Why was she letting him do this? She was weak, that was why. Where he was concerned, she had never exercised any willpower. She did foolish, irresponsible things; she acted rashly and paid later. Hadn't she grown up any? Hadn't she learned her lesson yet? Was she going to sacrifice her independence for the sake of a few kisses? No!

She pushed him away. He didn't release her, but lifted his head and stared down into her turbulent eyes. "Still mad at me? Why don't you tell me what I did?"

"I was never mad at you."

"Oh, I see. You left because you *weren't* mad at me."

"I don't want to play word games, Riley. And even if I did, I can't now. Do you realize I have a houseful of people who—"

"Do you still keep your secret cache of peanut M&Ms?"

"What!" Exasperation and surprise went into her exclamation.

"Now, don't pretend you don't know what I'm talking about," he chided. "That little basket of M&Ms you always hid in the pantry."

"I did not!"

"You did too," he countered, laughing and tweaking her nose. "Because you didn't want me to know you were snitching them once you'd sworn off chocolate."

"You were snitching them too!" She blushed to a bright crimson when she realized that she had admitted her own guilt.

While they were talking, Riley had been searching through the shelves of canned goods and cannisters of rice and pasta. "Uh-huh!" He gave a triumphant cry as his hand lighted on the telltale basket of candy, hidden behind two cans of grapefruit juice. He brought forth the basket and popped one of the M&Ms into his mouth. Before Brin could deflect his hand, he forced one between her lips.

"Why didn't you tell me you knew?" she asked sulkily.

"You knew I knew. Didn't you?" He asked the soft, prodding question with such an endearing grin, she couldn't resist smiling back.

"Yes. Why did we pretend it was a secret?"

"Because the game was so much fun. We didn't want to spoil it." The mischievous spark in his eyes mellowed to a steady blue flame. "We had a lot of fun, Brin."

"A lot of problems too."

"Most marriages do. I wasn't aware that we suffered an inordinate number."

"I know." She spoke quietly, lowering her gaze. "They were my problems, not yours," Brin confided.

"So you suffered in silence. Why didn't you talk to me about them?"

"I don't want to discuss it." She reached for the doorknob and pulled on it. The door didn't budge. Riley's hand was splayed wide on it, holding it closed.

"*I* want to discuss it, dammit."

"This is not the time."

"It's past time. It's been seven months! I want to know, and I want to know now, why my wife, my bride, walked out on me."

His temper flared. It frequently did. His fury might terrorize cameramen and engineers, even station managers, but Brin had learned early in their relationship not to give way. She certainly couldn't quail beneath it now. Though he dwarfed her physically, she faced him with matching belligerence. "I refuse to talk about it. It wouldn't do any good."

"This 'problem' is one we couldn't work out, is that it?"

"Yes! Something like that."

"I don't believe that."

"Take my word for it."

"Another man? Is it another man?"

"No."

"What else could it be? What else would be so final that it couldn't be worked out?"

"You're way off track, Riley."

"Abel Winn?"

"What?"

"Did you leave me for Abel Winn? Did you leave me to sleep with him?"

She slapped him. Hard. It was the first time either of them had ever struck the other. Brin was shocked to see her hand print form on his cheek. If her palm hadn't been stinging like a million pinpricks, she wouldn't have believed she had done it. A trickle of fear ran through her when she considered what Riley might do in reprisal.

But instead of getting angry, he smiled. He knew from her violent reaction that his accusation couldn't be true. He felt a vast sense of relief. A knot of misery began to unravel in his chest. The thing he had dreaded most didn't exist. Brin's reason for leaving him wasn't love for another man. He had sought her out tonight prepared to do anything to get her back. Make any compromise. Heal any hurt. But if she had loved another man, especially one as wealthy and powerful as Winn, it would have been hopeless.

His smile made her forget her momentary fear and only served to enflame her more. "How dare you say something like that to me?" she hissed. "I was faithful to you. That you could think . . . Oh!" She yanked on the doorknob, and this time he let her go. But as she left the pantry he was half a step behind her.

"You always were your most adorable when you were mad," he taunted. "You were mad the first day we met, remember?"

"No."

He gripped her upper arm and spun her around to face him. She landed against his chest, head thrown back, throat arched, breasts heaving. "The hell you don't," he growled. Then he kissed her soundly.

"Well, honestly," Stewart said from the doorway, "every time I catch you two alone you're in a clench. What's going on? Are you making it or not?"

Brin extricated herself from Riley's arms and left him to make their excuses to Stewart. She reentered the dining room and made a beeline for the bar, hastily pouring herself a glass of chilled white wine. Striving for composure, she moved away before Riley resumed his post at the bar.

*That man!* she fumed silently. His ego would make a case study. His nerve . . . well, it went beyond description. He thought that after seven months of separation he could just waltz into her house, lock her in a pantry, and without so much as a "How have you been, Brin?" kiss her the way he had.

She smiled placidly at her guests, who seemed not to have noticed that she had been missing. Abel had. When her eyes locked with his, they were inquiring. She suddenly wondered if her hair had been mussed by Riley's eager hands. Were her lips as red and pulsing as they felt? Were her clothes disarranged? In just those few minutes in the pantry Riley had been able to arouse her to a feverish pitch. Was it visible on the outside?

Pasting a false smile on her face, she engaged the gregarious couple standing next to her in conversation about their three-month-old daughter.

But Brin couldn't keep her mind on feedings and

diapers and pediatricians. It seemed determined to wander back to that day Riley had reminded her of, the one when she first met him. . . .

It was Brin's first day on the new job, and she was justifiably nervous as she made her way from her assigned space in the parking lot to the back door of the studio, where she would be admitted by a guard when she presented her pass.

"You've taken on a tremendous amount of responsibility," the personnel manager had warned her several days earlier. "He's not an easy man to work with. Artistic temperament, you understand."

She understood. Artistic temperament, my foot. Jon Riley was afflicted with the star syndrome. It was a unique disease that caused suffering in anyone caught in the tyrannical path of the afflicted. "I have every confidence that I can work with Mr. Riley," she had said assuredly.

The personnel manager cleared his throat. "Yes, well . . ." His expression was skeptical. "We've tried out several producers, both men and women, for *Riley in the Morning.* We haven't hit on the right combination of talents and personalities yet."

"You mean Mr. Riley's temper tantrums have scared the others off." The man's brows had jumped high in surprise at her bluntness. "I won't be so easily gotten rid of."

Brin only hoped she could maintain that level of confidence, as she made her way down the dank, dim hallway, which smelled of stale cigarette smoke and seemed characteristic of the two television studios where she had worked prior to taking this job.

She heard the shouting and weeping before she even shoved open the padded door and entered the cavernous studio. It was like stepping into the Mad Hatter's tea party without properly preparing oneself, or possibly entering the lions' cage without a whip or chair. Either way, the chances of survival seemed remote.

"Where was your head? Huh? Never mind. Let me hazard a guess." The guess that the man—Brin immediately recognized him as Jon Riley—made was obscene, and she winced when he voiced it. "You've done stupid things before, ignorant, asinine things, but this tops it! This is the great, big granddaddy of screw-ups!" He ran his hand through his hair and paused for breath.

The victim of this verbal flagellation was a woman who appeared to be in her early twenties. She stood in front of Riley with her face buried in her hands, shoulders hunched, sobbing wetly and noisily.

Assorted members of the crew reacted differently to the argument. One cameraman, his arm negligently flung over the end of his expensive camera while a cigarette dangled from his lips, looked for all the world like he was watching a play and enjoying it immensely.

A girl wearing jeans, sweat shirt, and sneakers was sitting on the concrete floor with her legs folded Indian fashion, chewing gum for all she was worth and occasionally blowing bubbles. Two young men were held in thrall by the pages of an issue of *Penthouse* magazine. Another, the most amazing of all, was sound asleep, his chair propped against the wall on its two back legs.

Riley paced back and forth in front of the crying young woman, shooting poison glances in her direction. He spat out his words like bullets from a machine gun. "What am I supposed to do? How do you suggest I get this straight? We've got a show to get on tape. It airs tomorrow. *Tomorrow!* And I'm surrounded by morons like you who can't even . . ." He stopped, running out of either vituperative words or breath. Brin wasn't sure which.

The young woman took advantage of his pause. "The new producer is supposed to be here today. Maybe she can calm her down."

"She, she, she. What producer? They've no doubt hired some deb whose tits are bigger than her brain. Spare me another producer. *You* were supposed to be acting as producer, and look what a fiasco you've managed to pull off."

"I'm sorry. I . . . I don't know—"

"Exactly."

The girl wailed and covered her face again. Brin had heard all she could stand. She took the steps necessary to bring her into the pool of light in the otherwise unlit studio. "Excuse me."

The star of *Riley in the Morning* whirled around and stabbed her with the bluest eyes she'd ever seen. They were legendary. Brin could see immediately why they were worthy of every comment she'd ever heard about them.

The victim of Riley's abuse stopped crying long enough to look up at Brin, a ray of hope shining in her tear-filled eyes.

A long gray ash fell from the cameraman's cigarette as he lazily shifted it from one side of his mouth to the other.

The sleeping man's chair hit the floor as he came awake abruptly, probably because a quiet, calm voice in that studio was as jarring as a fire alarm somewhere else.

Her voice had also called attention away from the *Penthouse* centerfold. Two pairs of eyes peered at Brin over the edge of the magazine.

The girl sitting on the floor stared up at Brin over her burst bubble.

"Don't tell me. Let me guess." Riley, standing arrogantly, with his hands propped on his hips, gave her a cursory once-over.

"That's right, Mr. Riley. I'm the deb with bigger tits than brains." Someone snickered. Someone else coughed. Riley's blue gaze dropped to her chest. Brin stood her ground. "As you can see, they aren't impressively large. I assure you my gray matter is. Would anyone care to tell me what's going on?"

They all started talking at once. Brin held up both hands. "Mr. Riley first, please, since he seems to be the most upset."

"I never get upset, Miss . . .?"

"Cassidy. If you'd seen fit to be present at my interview, you'd know my name, Mr. Riley. We could have had a production meeting then, and possibly this fiasco, as I heard you refer to it, could have been avoided." Score one for her.

"I leave at two every afternoon," he said without a flicker of warmth in his cold blue eyes. "Your interview wasn't until four. I wasn't about to hang around for two hours."

"But if you had," she said sweetly, "you wouldn't be ranting and raving this morning, would you?"

"Now, just a minute—"

"If I overheard correctly, we don't have a minute to spare," Brin snapped. "Do you want to get that show of yours on tape, or not? Tell me the problem. Let's fix it. Then if you want to tear into me you can, when we both have the time."

He gnawed the inside of his cheek, rocking back and forth slightly on the balls of his feet, looking like a man about to explode. Brin calmly stared him down. Finally he started talking in short, angry bursts.

"Dim Whit, here, told my guest—who happens to be a flaming freak with pink hair—to be here an hour before she was supposed to be. She is furious for having to wait while we set up. We've practically locked her in a room to keep her from screaming the building down. She's behaving like a lunatic, almost hysterical."

"That seems to be the general condition around here, from what I've seen so far," Brin remarked dryly.

Riley gave her a murderous look, but for the sake of time continued without comment. "The studio wasn't set up and ready for taping because *she*," he said, pointing to the cowering young woman, "forgot to put us on the schedule, which is already tight at best. In an hour we have to turn the studio over to production, because they're taping news promos this morning."

When his recital came to an end, Riley looked at her as if to say, "There. You asked for it; you got it. Now fix it." He looked almost satisfied. Smug. Daring her to respond.

Admiral Cassidy's daughter had never backed down from a dare.

Brin turned to the sniveling young woman Riley had referred to as Dim Whit. "What is your name?"

"Whitney," she said almost inaudibly.

"Whitney Stone, the sales manager's daughter, whom I've been appointed to wet-nurse through apprenticeship," Riley said.

"Shut up," Brin said, spinning around to face him. The cameraman whistled softly. The gum chewer nearly swallowed the wad in her mouth. "Your childish tirade wasn't helping much, was it?"

Before Riley could offer a rebuttal, Brin looked back at the girl. "Stop crying. That isn't doing us any good either. Now, the first thing I want you to do is get Mr. Riley a cup of coffee. I think he can use one. Then go upstairs to the control room and see if a director and sound engineer are available. If not, find them. Tell them I'm sorry the taping this morning wasn't scheduled and that I'll see to it a mistake like this never happens again. Got it?"

"Yes, ma'am." She fled the room as though escaping execution.

"You, you, and you," Brin said, pointing to three idle studio crewmen, "strike this news set and get Riley's ready."

"But the night crew's supposed to do that after the newscast. We—"

Brin glared at the objector. "Do it," she said succinctly.

They exchanged glances all around. The one who had been sleeping shrugged and pulled himself out of his chair. The others tossed down the magazine and ambled toward the news set, grumbling to each other.

"Put out that cigarette," she said to the cameraman. "You can't properly operate a camera with a cigarette either in your mouth or in your hand. No more smoking on this set. Is that understood?"

The man ignored her. "Hey, Riley, can she do that?"

Brin spoke up. "I can. I just did. If you don't like it, find yourself a job on another show. Just remember all those graduates of the video institutes who would love to fill your shoes. And you," she said looking down at the girl, who still had her legs folded beneath her, "keep the chewing gum in your mouth or you're off the set too. And while you're making up your mind, check out both Mr. Riley's microphone and one for his guest."

She turned to Riley, refusing to countenance the temper brewing behind those sapphire eyes. "Who is your guest for this show?"

"Pamela Hunn."

Pamela Hunn *did* have pink hair, and Brin was tempted to smile, but refrained, knowing that the way she played this hand might determine the outcome of the game. "Where is she?"

His chin jutted forward. "Dim Whit can show you." The young woman was just then crossing the studio, carrying the cup of steaming coffee like a peace offering. She stumbled over a cable and sloshed the coffee on the floor. Riley cursed beneath his breath. But he took the coffee from her with a gruffly spoken "Thanks."

"I suggest you put on some makeup, Mr. Riley," Brin said, hoping Whitney hadn't heard Riley's unkind epithet. "I'll come for you when we're ready. Do you have any material on Ms. Hunn?"

"Some," he replied curtly.

"Shouldn't you be studying it?"

With that terse suggestion she left the studio, asking Whitney Stone to show her where they had sequestered the enraged Pamela Hunn. She was a designer of haute couture, who had become immensely popular in recent years because her clothes were worn by the female lead of a weekly television series.

When Brin opened the door to the "green room," which in this instance was actually dirty beige, she was confronted by a woman whose face was almost as florid as her fuzzy hair. She had colorless beady eyes under a prominent brow. Her thin nose was pinched even tighter by fury.

"I demand an explanation for this outrage. I've never . . . well, I can't even begin to tell you how this has . . . Insult of the highest caliber, that's what it is."

She sputtered the words through lips that were perpetually pursed. When she realized she was speaking to someone she hadn't seen before, she stopped long enough to survey Brin haughtily. "Who are you? That's one of my blouses."

Brin thanked whatever angel was responsible for her having chosen to wear this particular blouse on this particular day. She could have chortled when Riley had told her who the offended guest was because she knew she would have an ace in the hole in dealing with her.

"My name is Brin Cassidy, and yes, this is one of your designs, Ms. Hunn. I saved my money for months to buy something with your label in it, and I can't tell you how much I love my blouse."

Pamela Hunn sniffed. "It's a gorgeous garment, of course. It would be on anybody, but you wear it exceptionally well. Size six? Four, maybe. The fabrication was inspired. The sleeve fairly flows with every movement, but it wouldn't have if I hadn't insisted that it be cut just so."

For several seconds she studied her creation with unabashed pride, then she sniffed again, as though she'd smelled something unpleasant. "You haven't said who you are in this menagerie. I'll have you know, young woman, that I have been a guest on Johnny Carson's *Tonight Show*, *Good Morning America*, *60 Minutes*, and *The Merv Griffin Show*. I've never, *never* been treated so shabbily. This is positively the garbage can of television shows. The armpit of—"

"You're absolutely right, Ms. Hunn. I couldn't agree with you more. If I were you, I'd refuse to do the show and storm out. Why should you subject yourself to a television interview after the way you've been treated? Why do them any favors? Imagine, you, the virtuoso of American designers, being handled like an ordinary guest, like an . . . an *actress* or something. Don't they realize you're an artist?"

Brin drew herself up as though she had had her say. In a quiet, deferential tone she asked, "Shall I call you a cab? Or did you come by limousine?"

"I . . . I . . . uh . . . drove myself. Occasionally I like to. Only occasionally, you understand. For recreation."

"Of course. Come, Ms. Hunn, let me usher you out. We've kept you entirely too long, and your time is so extremely valuable. Is that a portfolio of sketches? Don't forget it. How unfortunate that the audience will be denied seeing your designs because of the incompetence of the imbeciles around here. Stupidity is rampant on all levels of society, isn't it? Even in the fashion industry, I'll bet."

She was walking smartly at Pamela Hunn's side, praying that she was taking the right hallway toward the exit of the building. The intersecting corridors were an unfamiliar labyrinth, and she wondered what explanation she would give Pamela Hunn if she took a wrong turn straight into a broom closet. Her heart was hammering. Would her bluff work?

She smiled at the designer. "Didn't I read that you're doing an exclusive fashion show here in the Bay Area?"

"At Neiman's, yes. Tomorrow."

"How wonderful! Maybe I'll be able to attend. I only hope *someone* does."

The high heels of the designer's pointed-toe European shoes virtually screeched to a halt. "Why wouldn't they come? Why wouldn't I and my fashions draw a crowd?"

"Well, Ms. Hunn, *Riley in the Morning* has a large viewing audience, even if it is incompetently produced. But don't worry," she said, patting the other woman's rail-thin arm, "there'll probably be lots of women who'll see your fashion show publicized through another media."

"But—"

"And I didn't believe a word of what they said about Rachel Lamiel after she refused to do a local television show." She urged Pamela Hunn forward, but the woman didn't budge.

"Lamiel? She refused to do . . . What did they say?"

"Please," Brin said in a conspiratorial whisper. "You're asking me to be indiscreet."

"I won't tell anybody. What did they say about Lamiel?" Her skinny nostrils were quivering.

Brin glanced around with the wariness of someone about to impart a state secret. "They said that her designs were lousy and that she didn't want to advertise the fact before the fashion show was sold out. But as I said," she rushed to add, "*I* didn't believe that was the reason she flew into a rage and refused to go on television, as she had promised to do." She nudged the designer onward, hoping Pamela Hunn wouldn't guess that the tale she had just told was completely apocryphal. "Now, we've taken up far too much of your time, and I apologize for the error and the inconvenience we've caused you. I'll see to it—"

"Wait a minute." She wet her lips nervously and blinked furiously. "You really do look attractive in that blouse."

"Thank you."

"I would suggest a brighter color next time. The fuchsia, perhaps."

"Do you really think so?" Brin asked obsequiously.

"I didn't catch your name, my dear."

"Brin. Brin Cassidy."

"Well, Brin, you've been such an absolute doll that I've decided I'm going to do this tired little interview after all."

Brin spread her hand wide over her heart, which at that moment was pumping with glee. "Oh, Ms.

Hunn! What can I say? You're being far too gracious and forgiving."

"Please," the designer said, raising her hand as though granting a papal blessing. "That's part of being a professional."

By the time Brin led her into the studio, Pamela Hunn was practically purring. "Whitney, would you please get Ms. Hunn a cup of coffee? Cream or sugar?"

"Neither, my dear. We must watch our figures, you know." Brin laughed with her, while the crew looked on in stupefaction. "Sit here on this sofa, Ms. Hunn. So tacky, isn't it?" She looked toward the gum-chewing girl. "Careful how you attach her microphone. This blouse is silk." The designer missed the discreet wink she gave the girl.

Brin felt as if she had put in a hundred years rather than half an hour at her new job, but Pamela Hunn was situated on the set, wired for sound, and simpering under her adoration. It choked her to cater to an infantile ego, but if that would get this first interview on tape, so be it.

"How did you do it?" Whitney asked worshipfully as she led Brin to Riley's dressing room. "She called me a great, gawky girl totally without grace."

"At least she alliterated." When Whitney stared back at her blankly, Brin went on, "I stroked her ego."

Whitney stared at Brin with undiluted admiration. "You sure did a good job."

"Thanks. Speaking of egos, let's see what frame of mind Mr. Riley is in."

She knocked once on the door, but didn't wait for his permission before marching in. "We're ready for you on the set."

Riley was standing in front of the theater mirror, a towel tucked into his shirt collar. He was holding a sponge and a compact of base makeup in his hand; a small saucer of water and his coffee cup were on the dressing table. "You and I had better get something straight right now, Miss . . . what was it again?"

"Cassidy," she said tightly.

"Yeah, Cassidy." He turned from the mirror to face her. "*I* run the show around here. Nobody else. I let you get by with some high-handed maneuvers this morning because it was an emergency. But don't think that just because you can push other people on the set around, it includes me. Is that clear?"

Without releasing her from a glacial glare, he moistened his sponge, dabbed it into the compact of pancake makeup and spread some on the tip of his nose to cut the shine under studio lights.

Unperturbed by his warning and his intimidating stare, Brin calmly said, "We roll tape in two minutes, Mr. Riley. If you're not on the set by then I'll make a formal complaint to the production manager. And by the way, you just dipped your makeup sponge in your coffee."

She slammed out before he had a chance to speak. But she had to hand it to him: Furious as he was when he stormed onto the set, by the time the cameras were rolling, he was all pro.

Charm oozed. His voice held just the right amount of confidentiality, which had won the hearts of housewives pausing to watch his program between cycles of the clothes dryer, and secretaries clustered by the dozens around office coffee machines to gossip about him. If he didn't listen avidly to every word Pamela Hunn said, if he didn't have an earnest interest in the sketches the designer displayed and expounded upon, then he was a tremendous actor.

As soon as the show was in the can and Ms. Hunn had been escorted out, Brin called a production meeting for everyone associated with *Riley in the Morning*. Some of the crew's surliness had dissipated. Her handling of this morning's crisis had won her their respect if not their liking.

During the meeting she laid down a list of rules, regulations, and assignments, and firmly made it known that she expected them to be adhered to.

"You can be replaced." She was smiling when she said it, but her voice carried a discernible trace of threat. "*Riley in the Morning* is number two in the ratings during its time slot. By the next rating book, I want us to be number one and stay there. If you don't want to cooperate, get out now. Nothing is going to keep me from realizing my goal." As though on cue, her eyes slid to Riley. "I'd like to see you now in your dressing room, Mr. Riley."

Her heels tapped on the concrete floor as she left the studio and the properly subdued and silenced production crew. She was waiting in the hall outside his dressing room door by the time Riley caught up with her. He opened the door, bowed, and swept his hand wide, indicating that Brin should precede him. He followed her in and, without offering her a seat, flopped down on the sofa, working at the knot on his necktie. Brin remained standing in the middle of the room.

After consulting a notebook she said, "Every morning after the taping session is finished, Whitney will bring you a file on the next day's guest. Study the compiled information overnight. And from now on I won't tolerate any of your temper tantrums."

"You won't, huh?"

"No. I won't. And stop terrorizing Whitney."

"Dim Whit? She's used to it."

"For reasons I can't fathom, she adores you. But if she were a St. Bernard instead of a sensitive, impressionable young woman, I wouldn't let you talk to her the way you did this morning."

"You wouldn't *let* me?"

"What time did you go to bed last night?" she asked, as though he hadn't spoken.

"What?"

"You heard me."

He stared at her for a long moment. She watched his frown slowly reverse itself into a sly smile. "To *bed* or to *sleep*?"

She gave him a tired look and sighed. "I couldn't care less what goes on in your bed, Mr. Riley."

"Oh, no? Then why ask?"

"You force me to be blunt. You look like hell." She was rewarded by his dumbfounded expression. Apparently he wasn't accustomed to having his looks unfavorably criticized. "From now on get a good night's sleep before coming in to videotape the shows. And no wine the night before. It makes your eyes puffy."

He shrugged off his insouciance and sat up straight. "What the hell—"

"And if your eyes have bags under them anyway, I suggest you hold an ice pack on them for at least fifteen minutes every morning after you get up."

He wagged his index finger at her. "Let me tell you what you can do with your ice pack."

"I think that's all," she said, snapping her notebook closed.

"Not quite." He bounded off the sofa and caught her as she reached the doorway, gripping her by the shoulders.

"Release me."

A grin tugged at one corner of his lips. " 'Release me'? Didn't you forget the 'you cad'?"

"Let me go, Mr. Riley, or I'll—"

He burst out laughing. He laughed long and hard. His eyes were sparkling as they moved from the top of her head to the tips of her toes and back up. Jon Riley looked at his new producer, really looked at her, for the first time.

He saw a head of short, dark, curly hair, bobbed to just below her jaw. Dark brows arched gracefully over eyes the color of aquamarines, shot through now with sparks of anger. A pert nose. A kissable mouth. Oh, yes, a very kissable mouth, with a sulky lower lip he'd love to capture in a playful bite.

And most interesting of all, a shallow vertical cleft that nicked the edge of her chin and made it look damned impudent. She was cute and sexy and fiery, and if he hadn't made it an ironclad rule never to mix business with pleasure, he would see just how hot that fire inside her burned.

"You pack quite a wallop, don't you, Miss Cassidy?" he asked huskily after his laughter had subsided. "A tiny package of woman chock full of explosive dynamite. This is going to be interesting."

She worked herself free of his hands, and knew she succeeded only because he chose to let her go. She opened the door. "I'll see you in the morning, Mr. Riley."

"I wouldn't miss it for the world, Miss Cassidy."

The sound of his laughter had followed her down the hall that day. She had all but run from it, from him, because she had known, even then, that after having been touched, emotionally and physically, by Jon Riley, she would never be the same. . . .

# *Three*

"Earth to Brin. Come in, Brin."

"What? Oh, I'm sorry. I was—"

"I'll say. How can you daydream during a party? Some of us are ready to leave, but didn't think we should until we sing 'Happy Birthday' to the boss."

"Of course," Brin murmured, trying to pull her thoughts back into the present. "I'll speak with the caterer to see if the cake is ready."

She glanced at Riley on her way into the kitchen. He was still behind the bar, still dispensing drinks and grins, but his eyes were on her as she moved across the room. And from the intensity with which they burned, she suspected he knew where her thoughts had been.

Stewart was in the kitchen, already preparing to light the candles on the birthday cake. "I guess it's time for the cake," Brin said.

"I guess so," he said, snidely implying that he thought it was past time.

When all the candles were lit, Stewart held the swinging door open. Brin pushed the small wheeled cart into the dining room. Everyone turned and began applauding when they saw the spectacular cake. There followed a rousing chorus of "Happy Birthday" and Abel Winn was pushed forward through the crowd to blow out the candles, which he successfully accomplished in one breath.

He accepted everyone's hearty birthday congratulations and laughed good-naturedly at the jokes made about advancing age. Holding up his hands and begging for silence, he made a short speech.

"Thank you all for coming tonight and sharing my birthday with me. Those of you who have to work tomorrow . . . tough," he said bluntly, and everyone laughed. "There'll be no excuses for hangovers. You'll have Brin to blame for your excesses tonight. She is a hostess without equal." He turned to her and kissed her cheek affectionately.

Flustered, she asked Stewart to slice and serve the cake. Abel accepted the first slice, but drew Brin aside when everyone crowded forward to sample the dessert. Abel set the plate of cake on an end table when they managed to reach a semiprivate corner of the room.

"I meant what I said. Tonight's been special."

"I'm glad."

"And it's because of you, Brin."

Brin was aware that Riley was glowering at them from across the room. She smiled up at Abel brightly. "Thank you. It was my pleasure."

"I know this isn't the time to discuss business, but—"

"No, it really isn't, Abel," she said hastily as, from the corner of her eye, she watched Riley round the end of the bar and start making his way toward them.

"Please let me finish. Before you give me your answer tomorrow, I want to embellish our offer. How does forty thousand a year sound?"

"Extravagant." Too late. Riley was standing just behind Abel, looming over him like a dark bird of prey. Brin wondered why Abel didn't feel hot breath on the back of his neck.

"Perhaps it is a bit extravagant," Abel said, chuckling. "But I'm prepared to pay it to seduce you into accepting this job."

"You're too generous, and it sounds wonderful, but I still haven't decided." Didn't Riley have enough manners not to eavesdrop? Why didn't he go away? Why had he shown up at all, tonight of all nights, when her future hinged on this decision? She certainly didn't need Riley cluttering her mind.

"The second year you'll get a raise and start earning a percentage of the profits. Naturally, the company will cover all your moving expenses."

"I'm not too keen on moving to Los Angeles."

Winn frowned, thinking. "I want you to be happy. The company owns several houses down there. You can rent one from us for the cost of the utilities. There's one near the beach you might enjoy."

"Abel! I can't let you pay for my housing. Please, let's not talk about it any more tonight."

"But I must have your answer by tomorrow, and I

want to entice you into accepting. Tonight's my last chance."

"If I turn down the job, it's not because you haven't made the offer attractive enough."

"Very well," he said, looking disappointed. "I can see that you're a woman of integrity, who can't be bought. Talking about money unnerves you."

What unnerved Brin was seeing the malevolent expression on Riley's face. Abel must have noticed her absorption with something over his shoulder, because he turned around. "Oh, Mr. Riley. I'm trying to talk Brin into making a career change. You weren't very smart to let her go, you know."

Abel Winn smiled pleasantly into the threatening face frowning down at him, but the smile never reached his eyes. The atmosphere between the two men was as hostile as that between two male beasts competing for the favors of a female.

At last Abel said, "Brin, there's a group at the door waiting to say good night. Shouldn't we move over there?"

Without waiting for her compliance, Abel took her elbow and guided her forward. She had no choice but to go with him, and as hostess she should have been at the door anyway as the crowd began to thin out.

Still, she felt bad about deserting Riley, who looked so brooding and angry. And that sentimental feeling made her impatient with herself. Why should she care what Riley thought? She had left him months ago. In all that time he hadn't made any effort to contact her. Until tonight he'd been indifferent to their separation.

He was out of her life. Out of her system. And she was determined he remain out of both.

"You'll think about all I've said?" Abel asked as she held his coat for him half an hour later.

"I promise."

"And I'll have your answer tomorrow?"

"Yes."

Everyone but Stewart and his crew had left. She and Abel were alone at the door. He clasped her hands between both of his. "I know you'll give me the one I want," he said like a man accustomed to getting his way. "Good night, Brin. Everything was splendid." He kissed her cheek again, and she got the uneasy impression that with the least encouragement from her, he would have turned it into more than a fraternal peck.

Lord forbid! She had been down that road once. Mixing professional and personal relationships was deadly to the nerves, not to mention the heart and emotions. Never again. She had lived with one super ego, and, as much as she liked Abel Winn and respected his business acumen, she recognized an ego that would never enjoy sharing the limelight with anyone, especially a woman. Just like . . .

Riley? Quickly her eyes scanned the room. It was empty. Where was Riley?

She bade Abel a final good-bye, locked the front door, and went into the kitchen. Stewart was packing up the last of his supplies. The back door was standing open. Steve and Bart were loading a panel truck parked in her driveway. "Have you seen—"

"The hunk?" Stewart finished her question for her. "No. We were just lamenting that. He must have slipped out without even saying good-bye. Bart's simply crushed."

"Oh hush!" Bart mouthed as he hefted a crate of dishes to his shoulder.

Their bickering wasn't doing Brin's headache any good. She only wanted to be left in peace. And blessed silence. As she wrote out the check to cover Stewart's bill, she swore she wasn't disappointed that Riley had left just as abruptly as he had appeared.

"You forgot to deduct the fee for the bartender," Stewart said, looking at the amount of the check.

"Consider that your tip."

"You really are a doll. I hope we'll work together again." Stewart squeezed her shoulder before going out the back door and closing it behind him. Brin locked it and turned to face the littered kitchen. Stewart's fee didn't cover cleaning up her own dishes, and nothing was where it belonged.

She sighed, knowing she would never rest if she left the mess till morning. But before she tackled it, she was going to change her clothes. She hauled herself upstairs and entered her bedroom.

At the door she came to an abrupt standstill. Riley was stretched out on the bed, his head propped up against the headboard, casually thumbing through the latest issue of *Broadcasting*.

"Everybody gone?"

"What are you doing here?"

"Resting. Do you realize I was on my feet for almost four hours straight?"

"You know what I mean," she cried angrily. "What are you doing here? In my bedroom. On my bed. I thought you'd gone home."

"Home?" he asked, tossing the magazine aside.

"I don't have a *home*. I have a *house* that used to be a home . . . when I shared it with my wife."

She turned away from him, kicking off her shoes. Facing the mirror, she ran her hands through her hair. "I'm tired."

"You look it. Come lie down." He patted the space beside him on the bed. In the mirror he looked as tempting as the apple must have looked to Eve, and just as dangerous.

"Not on your life."

He laughed. "Why? Because you remember how much fun we had when we used to come home from parties?"

Exactly. And if she did cross the room and lie down with him, they'd make love, and then she'd be in the same rut as before. She couldn't survive the climb out of it again. The first time had nearly killed her. "I don't remember."

"Yes, you do. That's why you're afraid to lie down beside me. I wonder why it's so much fun to make love after a party. Is it because you're relaxed and usually in a good mood? We had some of our best times in bed after a party."

"Why won't you leave me alone? I've told you I'm not going to talk about this tonight."

"Do you still have that black lacy garter belt you wore when you dressed up?"

She whirled around, wondering if he could see through her clothes. "No."

He flashed a knowing smile. "Liar. You've got it on now."

"I do not!"

"Prove it."

"No."

He started laughing, and she ducked into the

bathroom to keep him from seeing her own smile. "What are you doing?" he called.

"Changing clothes."

"That's silly, isn't it?"

"What? Changing clothes?"

"No, taking cover to do it. I've seen you, you know. There's not an inch of your glorious skin that I can't describe in vivid detail."

In the bathroom, Brin unzipped her dress and peeled it down. She glanced at the garter belt around her hips and smiled. It had always stirred him to passion, though he'd never needed much titillation. The evocative words he called through the door brought a rosy blush to her skin.

"I'll bet you're wearing those panties that match the garter belt, aren't you?"

She shoved that very scrap of satin and lace down her legs and stepped out of the garment. "No."

"I can just imagine you standing there in those sheer black stockings."

She rolled them down her legs with careless speed. Cursing herself for a fool for even playing this childish game with him, she finished stripping until she was naked. Hastily she pulled on another pair of panties, an old pair of jeans, and a sweat shirt. After shoving her feet into a pair of moccasins, she went back into the bedroom.

"Charming," he said blandly.

"If you don't like my attire, you can leave." She stalked past the bed on her way to the door. He lunged off the bed and caught her by the seat of her pants. She screeched, but couldn't escape his grip in time, and found herself thrown across the bed on her back, with him stretched above her. He was grinning as he pinned her down.

"Let me up."

"Uh-uh. You get a certain glint in your eyes when you're feeling prissy and need to be taken down a notch or two. Give you an inch and you'll take a mile." He nuzzled her ear. "I'd like to give you a lot more than an inch, Brin."

"That's vulgar."

"Damn right, and you used to love it. The naughtier I talked, the better you liked it."

"I—Oh, stop." He had started tracking her ribs with his fingers. She was extremely ticklish. "Riley, I mean it now, stop!"

"Say please."

"Please," she gasped. "Please."

The tickling subsided, but his hand slid beneath the sweat shirt and stroked her stomach. "Bet you do have on those panties."

"Bet I don't."

"What do you bet?"

"Name it."

"A kiss?"

Sure of winning, Brin said, "You're on."

His blue eyes speared down into hers. She grew very still. He unsnapped her jeans and pulled the zipper down. His eyes skated down as he pushed the cloth aside.

He didn't see the black satin panties, but another pair just as sensuous, made of light blue silk. He closed his eyes as a wave of longing swept over him. When they came open again, he touched the smooth, soft skin of her abdomen.

"I win," Brin whispered shyly, suddenly submissive under the thoroughly masculine heat in his eyes.

"I welsh."

His hand slid over the silk panties, then inside them to the silk beneath. Making a low growling sound deep in his chest, he lowered his head. He kissed her navel, wantonly, hotly, relishing it with his tongue.

Brin was transported back, back to so many moments of passion such as this. She felt the familiar tendrils of desire twine through her system. Before she realized what she was doing, her hands were tangled in the silver-frosted strands of his hair, clasping and unclasping in a tempo that matched the gentle but thorough lashing of his tongue.

Her body was totally compliant, but her mind clung to a remnant of reason. "No, Riley, no."

"Oh, yes."

"No." She groaned with a mixture of frustration and arousal as he manipulated the spot he knew to be the most sensitive. "No!"

He lifted himself over her until his breath was striking her face in warm gusts. "Why? You want me."

"No."

"You *do*. You're my wife."

"Not anymore."

"There aren't any documents to that effect."

"It's not official, but—"

"All right, so you walked out. I let you go. I gave you space. Distance. Time. How long is this game of yours going to last, Brin?"

"It's not a game!"

"You won't let me make love to you?"

"No."

He rolled away from her, flopped onto his back, and covered his face with both hands. For long moments he lay there, breathing like a bellows, his chest heaving. He was still aroused. One glance at his tight-fitting jeans testified to that. Brin tore her eyes away, afraid that even now she might give in to what she wanted more than anything in the world, to have Riley inside her again. To hell with pride. She wanted Riley.

But he removed his hands from his face and rolled to a sitting position on the side of the bed. "No, I guess it isn't a game. A few hours, overnight, several days. That might be classified as a game. But not seven months. Whatever the reason you left me, it was serious, wasn't it?"

"Yes, very." She struggled to a sitting position and refastened her jeans, looking at him with troubled eyes. His smile was gentle and sad. He touched her cheek with the back of his finger.

"Let's go clean up the mess."

Taking her by the hand, he led her down the staircase. "I wish you would just go, Riley."

"Not yet."

"Please." Too many more scenes like the one upstairs and her icy resolve would thaw. It was dangerous to be around him. That was why she had made the separation quick and clean and absolute.

"Why do you want me to leave? Do you expect Winn back?"

She yanked her hand free of his. "No. I told you there wasn't anything like that between us."

"I saw you playing kissy-face."

"We weren't playing kissy-face."

"I saw him kiss you at least half a dozen times."

"Oh, for heaven's sake. He kissed me on the cheek a few times. Tiny tokens of appreciation."

"Yeah, well," he said, dumping ashes from a crystal ashtray into a plastic trash bag he'd taken from the kitchen, "I don't like other men kissing my wife, no matter how much they 'appreciate' her."

"Coming from you I find that laughable."

"What's that supposed to mean?" He loaded a tray with dirty glasses from the bar while she scooped up napkins and paper coasters and crammed them into the trash bag.

"It means that you've kissed your share of other men's wives. I don't remember a time we were out in public that some woman didn't come up and throw her arms around you. You always kissed back."

"That goes with my job."

"You didn't seem to mind it."

"Wait a minute!" He snapped his fingers as though a light had just come on inside his head. He looked at her with genuine disbelief. "Is that what this is all about?"

"What?"

"The separation. You saw some broad kiss me, and that provoked you into moving out?"

"Don't be ridiculous, Riley," she said, vexed that he could think her so petty. "If that were it, our marriage wouldn't have lasted the fifteen months it did before I left."

Brin didn't want to pursue that train of conversation, so, as they entered the kitchen carrying the party debris, she asked, "Are you hungry? You didn't have much time to eat."

"I nibbled, but I could stand something." He opened the refrigerator and pondered its contents. "By the way, you never did thank me for saving your neck tonight."

She paused in the act of tying shut the filled trash bag. "Thanks, Riley," she said with soft sincerity.

He glanced over his shoulder and winked. "Just so you appreciate me." He came up with the makings for a ham sandwich. "I was glad to do it. And it was fun. I only wish it hadn't been a party in honor of Abel Winn. And another thing," he said, slapping a knifeful of mustard on the slice of rye bread, "I didn't like what he said about my letting you 'get away.' What was all that about moving expenses and rent-free housing? What kind of job is he offering you?"

"A very good one," she said honestly. "Did you try any of this shrimp?" She popped one into her mouth.

"What kind of job, Brin?" He wasn't going to let her change the subject.

"As producer of *Front Page*," she admitted quietly, not meeting his eyes.

Riley laid his sandwich back on the plate without having taken one bite. Going to the back door, he gazed out the window at the skyline of one of the most beautiful cities in the world. Tonight he didn't even see it. Sliding his hands, palms out, into the back pockets of his jeans, he whistled softly. "That *is* a very good one."

"I haven't accepted it yet," she said hurriedly. She felt an almost maternal need to protect him. Why, she didn't know. But she felt that this piece of information might bruise his ego irreparably.

"Why not?" he asked, spinning around.

"I'm still considering it."

"What's to consider? *Front Page* has been written up in every trade publication. It's being touted as the hottest thing on television since *The Tonight Show.*"

"It's got a long way to go before it gets there. It's not even in production yet. It's still on the drawing board. The concept hasn't been clearly defined. Talent hasn't been selected. They're not even market-testing people yet." She said that to let him know that he hadn't been entirely passed over as a possible candidate for a host position on the new show. "Abel is projecting that it'll be early next year before it goes on the air. And it'll be syndicated. There are no guarantees that stations will buy it."

"They'll buy it. It's got Winn's megabucks backing it. It'll be a slick package they'll scoop up like popcorn." He looked at her closely. "And he wants you to be its producer."

"One of several. A Hollywood veteran has been named executive producer."

"I repeat, what's to consider?"

"I like what I'm doing now," she said evasively.

"That two-bit radio show?" he asked incredulously.

"*I* don't think it's two-bit."

"For your talents it is. Anyone fresh out of a college communications course could handle it. You outclass that program, and you know it. Besides, you should be in television. Why are you stalling Winn? Holding out for more money?"

"No."

"Then I don't understand."

She moistened her lips. "I'd have to move to L.A., for one thing. You know I love San Francisco."

"It would mean leaving behind more than the city."

"Yes." She fiddled with the hem of a dish towel. "My parents."

"And me." Her head snapped up and her eyes clashed with penetrating blue ones. "Were you going to skip out of town without a word?"

"No. I was . . ." She swallowed hard. "I was going to ask for a divorce."

The silence that descended was deafening. When Riley broke it, his words sounded brittle enough to break. "Is that why you haven't asked for a divorce before? Because no job offer has been attractive enough until now?"

The accusation stung, but it was justified. That must be what it looked like to him, and Brin didn't blame him for jumping to that conclusion. If only he knew that he had been the main reason she hadn't accepted Winn's job offer immediately. She couldn't quite bring herself to think about making a final, irrevocable break with Riley.

She had lived without him for seven months, but they were still legally married. They still shared the same city, the same name. Taking the job with *Front Page* and moving to L.A. would end the state of marital limbo they were in and make divorce a necessity.

"I swear to you, one has nothing to do with the other," she said.

He came toward her slowly, searching her face, looking for clues to the problem that still perplexed him. "Why did you leave me, Brin? And why, if living with me and being my wife were so intolerable, why haven't you asked to be free of me completely?"

He cupped her face in his hands and tilted her head up. He stroked away her tears with the pads of his thumbs. "*Why?*"

"I don't know," she groaned. "No reason. A million reasons. It's all muddled up in my head."

He pressed his lips against her forehead, drawing her close and squeezing his eyes shut against the pleasure and pain of holding her, but not having her. "You haven't asked for a divorce because you don't want one. You don't want to be rid of me any more than I want to be rid of you. And I don't think you want that job, either, or you would have jumped at the chance."

"Don't you think I can handle it?"

He put space between them and smiled down at her. "I know you can. Do you think I've forgotten what you did for *Riley in the Morning*?"


Three months after she started working at the television station, they got the results of the rating period. *Riley in the Morning* hadn't quite made it to the number-one position in its time slot, but it was gaining substantially.

Brin allowed the crew one celebratory coffee break before calling a production meeting. She was a slave driver, a taskmaster, but instilled in all her subordinates a zeal for what they were doing.

Perhaps that was a skill she had learned from her father, a Navy man whose last post had been in San Francisco. The Cassidys had liked the cosmopolitan city so well that when Admiral Cassidy retired, they decided to stay. After having been moved all over the world during her childhood, Brin was allowed to attend her last three years of high school in one place.

The people she worked with knew little about her other than that she was a bundle of energy who pestered them with details until everything was perfect. Innovative ideas seemed never to be in short supply. The crew listened, fascinated but incredulous, as she suggested that they do some of the programs live and on location rather than restricting the show to the studio.

". . . with a live audience," she finished, her face expectant and excited.

"Live?"

"With an audience?"

Riley's response belonged on the piers.

"Well, why not?" she demanded, put off by their lack of enthusiasm for the idea.

"It's never been done before."

"That's a real good reason," she said dryly, giving the floor director a scornful look. "Thank God they didn't say that to Phil Donahue."

"All right, you've made your point, but what about money? It'll be expensive to transport all the studio cameras to an outside location. Not to mention the overtime it'll cost for engineers to set it up."

"Leave that to me," she said confidently. "If I can work out the details with management, are all of you game?" They nodded. The enthusiasm she had generated was infectious. "Riley?" she asked.

Their first few weeks of working together had been rocky. He'd scowled. She had looked through him. He'd grumbled. She had turned a deaf ear. He'd shouted. She had shouted back. Sometimes they had raised the roof with their arguments, but he had come to respect her judgment. She might look like a doll, but she was far from dumb.

"If you could get that freak with the pink hair to eat out of your hand, you can accomplish anything."

Four weeks later found them broadcasting the fifth and final show of the week live from a new shopping mall. Each morning they had drawn a live audience of several hundred. Everyone at the studio from the lowliest gofer to the CEO was high on the success of Brin's idea.

It had been a terrific week. Viewers had loved the change of pace, as their calls and letters testified. Everyone in the sales department was doing hand-springs, because sponsors were calling them, wanting to buy commercial time on *Riley in the Morning*.

Brin and Riley had been working closely together. She had ceased being strictly his producer and had become his wardrobe consultant, makeup artist, scriptwriter, and general right hand.

"Brin?"

"Hmm?" She was concentrating on placing the lavaliere microphone in just the right place on his necktie. It was only a few minutes before air time. Everyone else had cleared off the set. Brin had jumped up from her high stool behind camera one and bounded up on the dais to adjust the microphone more to her liking.

"If a union boss catches you doing that, he'll have your rear."

"Then let's hope no one catches me."

"Yeah. I'd sure hate to see anything happen to such a cute behind."

She took the compliment in stride. Such comments from coworkers were easy to come by and didn't mean anything. "I won't be but another second."

"Take your time. I rather like the feel of your fingers in my chest hair."

*That* meant something. And she couldn't have taken it in stride if her life had depended on it.

Her eyes sprang up to meet his. She was alarmed to find his face so close to hers. And her fingers *were* in his chest hair. She had slid them between the buttons of his shirt in order to adjust the mike cord so that it would remain as invisible as possible. Nervously she wet her lips with her tongue and noticed that he was watching her mouth as she did.

"There, I'm done," she said thickly, withdrawing her fingers quickly.

"Lunch?"

"What?"

"Lunch? Today? When we get finished here?"

"Uh, I don't think so, no."

"Dinner?" He grinned. Winningly. Boyishly. She heard someone in the front row of his audience sigh. A woman no doubt. As a result of his smile, Brin felt her thighs grow weak and fell prey to a melting sensation that was delicious . . . but alarming.

"Definitely not."

"Breakfast, then."

"I don't ever eat breakfast out."

"Neither do I." The soft emphasis with which he spoke set off a chain of explosions in her middle. Her eyes locked with his and there was no mistaking what his invitation to breakfast implied.

"Hey, Brin, baby," the head cameraman called out, "we've got a great view of your tush, but unless you want that to be our opening shot, you'd better haul your buns off the set. Counting down from thirty seconds."

She turned and ran. Literally. And not just to get off the set in time. But to escape the captivating power of Riley's eyes, his compelling voice, his seductive insinuations, and her treacherous susceptibility to all three.

For the last several weeks she had felt that she and Jon Riley had finally reached an understanding, had established a reasonably good working relationship, had even formed some kind of grudging friendship. And yes, in quiet moments, when she wasn't being observed by either him or the crew, she had looked at him as most women would and had seen an attractive, sexy, virile male. What woman wouldn't notice and admire?

But *this! This* was out of the question. *This* was to be avoided at all costs.

Still, after the broadcast, she secretly hoped he would seek her out and continue the forbidden conversation. She would never accept a date, of course, but it was nice to be pursued.

But as soon as the cameras were shut down, he was surrounded by adoring fans, all clamoring for his autograph. One aggressive female fan nearly wrenched his neck in her effort to smack a kiss on his mouth. He only laughed and let her indulge herself.

"Brin?"

"What?" She was unaccountably furious, and spun around at the sound of her name. Whitney Stone jumped back in fright. Only then did Brin realize her fists were clenched at her sides. "I'm sorry, Whitney. What is it?"

"I'm spreading the word. We're all going to lunch

together as soon as everything's packed up. Daddy's footing the bill on behalf of the station. It's a celebration." She named the restaurant and Brin nodded in agreement.

But she didn't go. She told herself it was because her desk was piled high with papers, that she had mounds of work to do back at the station, phone calls to return, letters to answer. But actually it was because she was fuming, boiling mad, and she couldn't say why. Or, rather, she *could*, and that was the real reason behind her anger.

She refused to believe she was jealous of every woman who made a fool of herself over Jon Riley. *She* would certainly never fall into the ranks of his adoring fans.

Her mood didn't improve when Riley came crashing into her office without even knocking. He slammed the door behind him. "Where were you?"

She catapulted out of the chair behind her desk and faced him belligerently. They squared off like two fighters in the ring. "If you need me for something having to do with the show, I'd appreciate—"

"Where the hell were you? Dim Whit said she told you where we were meeting for lunch."

"She did. I chose not to go." For no good reason, she slammed a file drawer shut. It broke her nail, and she cursed.

"Why?"

"I didn't want to."

"*I* wanted you to."

"I doubt you even missed me. I'm sure there were plenty of fans there drooling over you."

He stared at her for a moment, then slapped the heel of his hand against his forehead. "My God, she's jealous."

"What!" Brin shrieked. "Me?" Her eyes narrowed to slits. "Why you pompous, conceited, arrogant buffoon. I wouldn't give you—"

A gentle push sent her up against the wall. His shove had enough impetus behind it to knock the breath out of her and give him the advantage. He trapped her between himself and the wall.

"What you give me is a hard time and a hard—" His hips pressed forward, making his meaning abundantly clear. "You're the most maddening, aggravating, infuriating female I've ever had the misfortune to meet. The most irritating, exasperating"—his voice lowered—"exciting . . . oh, hell."

His mouth came down hard on hers. She fought him like a wildcat, squirming and wriggling, clawing and slapping when she could get her hands free.

He was stronger. He was male. Unrelenting in his purpose. Driven by need. His lips twisted over hers, parting them. His tongue plunged inside.

Brin's squeals of outrage eventually softened to whimpers of defeat, then, at the coaxing of his tongue, to sighs of desire. When she stopped struggling, he lifted his hands to either side of her face and tilted her head back. His mouth gentled considerably. His lips tempered from plunder to persuasion. His tongue no longer thrust bruisingly, but sank with delicious leisure and thoroughness into the silky heat of her mouth.

They kissed forever.

And when finally he raised his head, he looked down into eyes as confused and cloudy as his. "Dammit, Brin," he whispered hoarsely. "What did you do to me? What's going on here?"

# Four

The silence in the kitchen was so profound that the drip in the sink sounded like Niagara Falls.

"That first kiss knocked me for a loop," Riley whispered huskily in her ear, knowing that she had been sharing his memory whether she ever admitted it or not. "I had never tasted anything so delicious as your kiss. I couldn't get enough of your mouth. I'd had climaxes that didn't effect me nearly that much."

"Riley, please." Brin felt herself weakening again. Damn his glibness! He was a master at ad lib. He knew what to say, and how to say it seductively. No wonder that honeyed tone and lilting inflection had kept him king of the morning talk shows for years. His female audience couldn't resist them.

But he wasn't an image on a television screen and she wasn't an audience of one. This was real.

"Thinking about the past isn't doing either one of us any good." She pushed him away and busied herself at the counter top.

"Coward."

She turned on the hot-water tap full force. A cloud of steam blossomed around her as she glared at him. "I'm not a coward."

He laughed. "You wouldn't have made Admiral Cassidy very proud of you that day. He would have shot any man in his Navy who showed such cowardice."

"I wasn't afraid of you, Riley."

"Not of me." He touched the tip of her nose. "Of yourself. And of what was happening to you on the inside. Here." His finger slid down her front and softly poked her just below the navel.

She swatted his hand away. "I merely left the office."

"You ran like a scared rabbit."

"If you'll remember right, I was called away. I got a summons from the station manager." Viciously she squirted a stream of liquid soap into the sink.

"Yeah, I remember. Dim Whit knocked on your office door with the message just as I touched your breast. I never have forgiven her for that," he said wryly.

"I thank heaven she timed it so well. I don't know what came over me."

"*I* would have if she hadn't interrupted." His mischievous grin and the expression in his eyes left no doubt that the double-entendre was intentional.

Brin was suffused with heat, as though her body

had been stroked by the devil. "Nothing like that would have happened at work. We both have better sense than that."

He began placing dishes in the dishwasher after she had rinsed them in the soapy water. He chuckled. "Brin, honey, you're still an innocent. Write this down as fact. If Dim Whit hadn't knocked on your office door at the precise moment she did, I would have done my damnedest to get inside your clothes, to get inside you. Right then. Right there. I didn't even know where I was. And it didn't matter. I had to have you. Had to kiss you. Yes, I have better sense than to do anything like that at work, but common sense was shot to hell the minute I touched you."

He turned to her, and she was consumed by the blue flame in his eyes. Beneath the heap of bubbles in the sink, her hands fell still. "I was so angry because you hadn't joined us for lunch that I could have wrung your neck. But I simply had to kiss you. It wouldn't have mattered if the sky had opened up and rained down fire on me, or if Satan had reached up out of Hell and grabbed me by the ankles, I had to kiss you."

She dragged her eyes away from his. But she couldn't close off her ears. When he spoke again, the words descended on her like velvet caresses. "I knew I was in love with you after that first kiss."

He stepped away from her, and the emotional vise squeezing her chest relaxed. She admonished herself for letting him get to her this way. He played with her emotions. She mustn't let him. For whatever reason, he had decided he needed her, after seven months. But as soon as his ego was soothed, as soon as she had served his immediate purpose, she would be right back where she'd started.

"You didn't finish your sandwich," she remarked, hoping to distract him.

"I'll get around to it," he said offhandedly, as though his mind were elsewhere. He was sitting on a kitchen stool. The heels of his shoes were hooked over the bottom rung. "I think that's when you knew you loved me too."

Her diversionary tactic hadn't worked. He seemed to have a one-track mind. Well, if he could rehash their past without its causing him unbearable pain, couldn't she? If she avoided talking about those golden days, wasn't that as good as an admission that she still cared? Damned if she would let him think that.

"How did you reach that conclusion?" she asked with studied nonchalance.

"You started avoiding me after that."

"Hardly. I saw you every day."

"In production meetings and on the set. But if we so much as accidentally met at the coffee vendor, you scuttled away."

"I've never scuttled in my life."

"You know what I mean. You wouldn't risk being alone with me for ten seconds."

"Because every time we were, you tried to grab me."

"You enjoyed being grabbed."

She blushed, knowing there was no sense in denying that. "Someone could have seen us."

"I had to chance it. I was desperate to get my hands on you."

"Oh, sure. As I remember it, you were squiring that football player's widow at the time."

"I had to keep up appearances. What did you expect me to do, have it leaked to the press that Jon Riley had the hots for his producer? Besides, if I had asked you out, you wouldn't have gone. Right?"

"Right. But you got around that, didn't you?"

He shrugged. "I had no choice but to trick you."

His grin was so disarming, she had to smile back. "I should have seen straight through your ruse."

"I think you did," he suggested smugly.

"No I didn't!" She denied it vehemently, though she had often wondered if she had known what he was up to that day he called. . . .


"Hello?"

"Hi, Brin. What are you doing?"

The nerve! The conceit! To call and not even identify himself. "Who is this?" she asked perversely.

"I'm sorry. This is Jon Riley," he said formally. She heard the amusement overriding his tone and wished she had held her tongue. She'd only given him rope to hang her. "Are you busy?"

"Yes."

"Doing what?"

"Cleaning my apartment."

"Can it wait ?"

"No."

"I want you to meet me."

"Now?"

"Sure, now."

"Forget it."

"Why?"

"I don't want to."

"But I have a terrific idea that won't wait."

"It'll have to. This is Saturday. I'm off on Saturdays. We'll talk about it at the production meeting on Monday."

She made herself sound piqued and impatient, but her heart was chanting, "Don't hang up yet, don't hang up yet," and her fingers were nervously twisting the phone cord. Her pulse was drumming double time and her palms had grown moist. And those were only the physical manifestations she allowed herself to acknowledge. Others were too embarrassing to think about.

"I'm in the park." He said it as though that explained everything.

She glanced out her window. "The park? On a day like today? It's cold, and I think it's going to rain."

"Nonsense. How soon can you be here?"

*Tell him to go to hell,* her better judgment warned her. "I haven't agreed to meet you."

"Do you want to hear this idea or don't you? What kind of producer are you?"

"An underpaid one."

"You just got a raise. You were given three months to prove yourself. When the last rating book showed a marked increase in our viewership, you got a raise. Want me to be really gauche and tell you how much it was?"

"How do you know all that?" she asked, aghast.

"Dim Whit overheard her dad talking about it."

"Does she report everything to you?"

"As you said, she adores me." His arrogant grin transmitted itself through the telephone.

"You really are a manipu—"

"How soon can you be here?"

"I haven't said I'm coming."

"But you are, aren't you?"

*No. No. No.* But her mouth seemed incapable of forming that simple one-syllable word. Instead she heard herself grumbling, "Oh, all right. But only for a while. Where are you?"

Every step of the way she told herself to slow down; she didn't want to be early or seem too anxious to see him. In spite of her determination to appear unhurried, she arrived at Golden Gate Park in record time, breathless and expectant. But he wasn't at the appointed place, a public telephone booth, where he had said he would meet her. Damn him! Well, she certainly wasn't going to loiter about as though she were waiting for him.

Her attention was called to a spontaneous frisbee-throwing contest being held on one of the famous park's grassy fields. One contestant was matching the skills of his Doberman with those of a red Irish Setter. The agile dogs and their masters had drawn quite a crowd. Brin wandered through it, willing her eyes not to search every face to find Riley's.

*"Pst!"*

She turned her head, but quickly continued on her way. The man who had so rudely addressed her was unshaven and had a slouchy fedora pulled down low over his brow. He was wearing opaque sunglasses in spite of the gloomy clouds overhead. If he had been wearing a trench coat instead of the leather bomber jacket he had on, Brin might have thought he was a flasher. As it was, he was merely a creep.

*"Pst!"*

Glancing over her shoulder, she was alarmed to see that the creep was following her. "Get lost." A woman alone wasn't safe anywhere these days!

"Playing hard to get, Brin?"

She stumbled on her own two feet as she whipped around and peered at the face behind the hat and beard stubble and sunglasses. "*Riley?*"

"Shh." He flipped up the sunglasses long enough for her to see the eyes that could only belong to him. "It's me." He took her hand and steered her away from the crowd, still watching the frisbee contest.

"What are you doing? Why are you dressed like that? I didn't recognize you."

"Which is precisely the point. When I go out on Saturday mornings I don't want to be recognized."

He was hustling her across the grass so fast she could barely keep up with his long stride. "I thought you were a masher."

"I am," he said, grinning down at her. "I got the girl, didn't I?"

"Where are we going?"

"Into the woods."

She tried to stop, but he dragged her along. "I thought this was a business meeting."

"Who told you that?"

"You did."

"No, I didn't. I said I had an idea to discuss with you."

"Well, that could only mean—Ouch! Slow down. I got the backlash of that branch."

"Sorry. Now, what were you saying?"

"I said"—she panted—"that you mentioned a great idea that couldn't wait till Monday. Can we rest, please?"

"Okay. It's starting to rain, anyway. Let's duck under here." He ran down a shallow ravine. She had no choice but to scramble after him. He pulled her beneath a footbridge just as the clouds opened up to release a soft, fragrant silver rain.

"Terrific," she said, staring out at the water-washed landscape. "I told you it was going to rain." Turning, she looked up at him with aggravation. "So here I am wasting a good day off by standing under a bridge in Golden Gate Park with you. Now, what brilliant idea of yours got me into this situation? And for heaven's sake, would you please take off those ridiculous glasses so I'll know for sure who I'm talking to?" He took off the sunglasses and put them in the pocket of his jacket. "Thank you. Now let's hear that idea."

"I think we should turn this into a meaningful relationship."

She stared at him blankly. Her expression didn't change. Her face didn't register the slightest emotion. When several seconds ticked by and she still didn't say anything, he said, "That's it."

"That's it? *That's it?* That's what you dragged me out of a nice, warm, dry, comfortable apartment on a Saturday morning to say?"

"Yeah!" he replied with a happy grin. "What do you think about it?"

"I think you're insane." She spun on her heel and took a step into the pelting rain, but he grabbed the hem of her jacket and jerked her back. His arms went around her securely, and she found herself locked in an embrace that felt too good not to terrify her.

He was strong, lean, hard, masculine. Her first impulse was to wrap her arms around him and get as close to him as she could. But that would be foolhardy, so she resisted the temptation. Instead she inclined away from him. He was having none of that and only drew her closer by tightening his arms around her.

"I think the idea merits some discussion, at least."

"It won't matter if we discuss it from now till doomsday, Riley. It's impossible."

"Nothing's impossible."

"This is."

"Why?"

"It would never work."

"Why?"

"We're business associates."

"So?"

"So we should keep it strictly business."

"Shut up."

"You're—"

"For once, Brin Cassidy, just shut up."

He bent his head low and captured her lips with his. And hers clung. She couldn't have denied herself that kiss in a million years, because his whiskers were about the most exciting thing she had ever felt against the delicate skin of her face. His lips were warm and moist as they moved to part hers. His tongue was darting and playful, and slow and deliberate, and thoroughly erotic, as it first skimmed the inner lining of her lips, then dipped far inside to fill the hollow of her mouth. He tasted like peppermint toothpaste and smelled like expensive cologne and rain . . . and man . . . and sex.

"God, Brin, I thought I'd die before I had a chance to kiss you again." He buried his beard-roughened face inside her collar and kissed her neck.

"This is crazy. Crazy." But even her own assessment of the situation didn't stop her from taking full advantage of being held in Riley's arms. She knocked the hat off his head onto the leaf-strewn ground. She nuzzled his ear and brushed her lips through the dark, silver-streaked hair just above it. "We shouldn't be doing this."

"But we are and it's fantastic."

"Hmm."

"Isn't it?"

"Hmm."

Their mouths fused again, and she marveled over the evocative powers of his kiss. She felt that kiss all the way down to her toes. It swirled around her breasts, through her belly, and into her thighs.

She slid her hands into his jacket, around his waist, and flattened them on the supple muscles of his back. "If we should be seen . . ." she said with a moan when their lips drifted apart to flirt with each other.

"We won't be. And even if we are—Ouch!"

"What's the matter?"

"Something . . . the zipper on your jacket, I think . . . There. Yes, that's better. Like that."

She sighed contentedly as he opened her jacket and pressed her against his chest.

He kissed her with a wildness that was thrilling, his head moving from side to side, his tongue probing as though searching for an entrance into her soul. "I want you, Brin. So damn much."

He cupped her bottom and lifted her off the ground, settling her against him in a way that banished any doubt as to his need. He fit their bodies together as nature had intended. The provocative grinding of his hips robbed her of breath.

"Please, please." She wasn't sure what she was begging for, but the words seemed to slip from her lips each time his mouth released them.

She lost count of the kisses they shared. Greedily her hands caressed him, and he took liberties with her until she was almost frantic with need. But somehow each of them retained a modicum of reason.

At last he let her slide down his body until her toes touched the ground again. She rested her cheek on his chest and heard the thudding of his heart. His hands moved lovingly in her hair. His lips brushed petal-soft kisses on her temple. The air was fogged with the moist vapor of their breath. . . .

"Sometimes I can still hear the way the rain sounded on that bridge overhead," he whispered now.

Emotionally overwrought, Brin leaned against the kitchen counter top, her arms stiffly bracing her up. Riley stood behind her. Close. So close she could feel his body's response to the memory of that rain-shrouded afternoon under the bridge. His hands rested on her hips, lightly, but with enough strength to hold her bottom against his front. His breath was warm and misty on her neck as he spoke softly.

"I wanted to make love to you right there. Lying in the leaves, standing up, any way I could. I wanted you so bad I ached." He kissed the back of her neck, opening his mouth and sponging her skin with the tip of his tongue. "Maybe I should have." His hands slid around to the front of her thighs. He moved them up and down, stroking soothingly, until they climbed to the top. His thumbs nestled in the grooves that funneled toward the vibrating heart of her femininity. "Maybe I shouldn't have let you talk me into taking things slow." His thumbs moved, and she gasped.

Breaking away from him, she put necessary space between them. "That was the only way it could be," she said in a trembling voice. "Then and now. You can't come sailing into my life after seven months of separation and pick up where we left off. I need space, time to sort things—"

"Oh, bull!" he shouted angrily. "All that space and time didn't do you any good the first time. You laid down the game rules and, like a puppy on a leash, I obeyed them. You insisted on only one official date a week. No hanky-panky at work. 'Keep it strictly professional at the TV station,' you said, and I did."

"Because you knew as well as I did that we couldn't compromise our jobs."

"Right. I agreed with that. But I went through weeks of pure hell until you finally admitted that you wanted me just as badly as I wanted you. You're so damned stubborn, Brin. I knew from that first kiss that we would be a perfect team, in bed as well as out. And in the long run I was proved right." He started laughing. "Of course you were *shocked* into admitting it."

"If you're referring to—"

"That's exactly what I'm referring to."

\* \* \*

"Come in," Brin called out.

Whitney stuck her head around the door to the producer's office. "Hi. Sorry to bother you, but we've got a problem."

"Just one?" Brin said, smiling. "What this time? Don't tell me Monday's interview has canceled."

"No, but Riley's already left, and he forgot to take his homework with him."

"Forgot?" Brin asked skeptically. He was so good at improvising during interviews that she had a heck of a time getting him to study pertinent facts before the cameras rolled.

"Well, in any event, I found the file on the set and he's split," Whitney said. "I'd take it to him, but I'm flying to Palm Springs with my folks for the weekend as soon as I get off work."

Brin took the file reluctantly. "I guess I could drop it off at his place." One of her stipulations had been that they avoid spending time in each other's homes. She didn't know how much longer she could hold out without going to bed with him, but she was bound and determined not to be just another notch on his infamous belt.

She waited until late that Friday evening before driving to his address, hoping that he would already have gone out and she could leave the folder in his mailbox. How she would bear the torment of learning that he was out with someone else she didn't know.

His sports car was parked in the driveway, however, and Brin moved toward the front door with the weak-kneed trepidation of a music student approaching the piano at her first recital.

She rang the bell, once, twice. She was just

about to leave the file in the mailbox and make a mad dash for her car when the door swung open.

"Oh!" Her hand flew to her chest, but she managed to avoid covering her eyes.

"Brin!" His delight couldn't be masked. "What are you doing here?"

"I, uh, brought you this." She thrust the file at him as if it were a hot potato. "Were you taking a shower?"

"No. I always walk around wet with a towel around my waist when I'm at home." His grin was heart-stopping. He looked devastatingly handsome, even if his hair was plastered to his forehead in sodden points. "Come on in," he offered, stepping aside.

Like a somnambulist, she moved inside. She was dazzled by his bare chest. The muscles dipped and curved appreciably, without looking grotesque. Last summer's tan had soaked into his skin, for there was still evidence of it. The network of hair covering it was dark and beaded now with drops of water that she could imagine catching on her tongue and swallowing. She avoided looking at the square of terry cloth that covered his loins, but his legs were long and lean and as athletically proportioned as the rest of him.

When her eyes finally returned to his face, her tongue felt too thick to form words. "I can't stay."

"Don't be silly. Besides, I'd like you to see my house."

At the risk of appearing rude at best and a prude at worst, she made no further move to enter, gazing instead at the spacious, tastefully decorated, plant-filled hallway, which had a skylight. When Riley closed the front door, the finality of that clicking, metallic sound brought her around as surely as smelling salts.

"I'm sorry for the intrusion," she said in a breathless rush. "I know you must be getting ready to go out. If it hadn't been important that I bring over the file, I wouldn't have bothered you on a Friday night. But you've got two very serious interviews to do on Monday and one of the topics you'll be discussing is abortion and you know how controversial that is, so I've compiled a lot of information and it will be necessary—"

"I love you, Brin."

She was stopped dead in her tracks.

Mutely, she stared up at him. She didn't speak, didn't even smile. It didn't strike her as ridiculous that he was standing in a puddle of water he'd dripped onto the floor. She was mesmerized by his eyes and the sincerity she read in them. For once, she merely stood there and listened.

"I'm not getting ready to go out. I was getting ready to spend a quiet evening at home, alone, thinking about you. Which is what I do to occupy just about every minute of the day."

He laid the folder she had given him on a table and took the steps necessary to bring them nose to nose. "I love you." Pressing her face between his hands, he granted her the sweetest kiss she had ever known in her life. Passion smoldered just below the surface, but this was a kiss of devotion, a tender expression of newfound love.

Calmly, almost with detachment, he unbuttoned her coat and slipped it off her shoulders. Unheeded, it fell to the floor. He touched the front of her blouse, lightly, barely skimming it with his hands. Then, without asking her permission, he unfastened the buttons. He was in no hurry. When all the buttons were undone, he spread the fabric wide.

His eyes made several rapid sweeps, then slowed to make a leisurely search, drinking in every detail of texture, shape, and color. He unhooked the fastener of her brassiere. She didn't deter him. The lacy garment came free, and he peeled it away.

Brin felt him stiffen. She saw him swallow hard. Saw him blink away tears. Saw him lower his head. Then she felt his mouth, warm and wet and loving. Loving her.

"I love you, I love you," he vowed against the silky skin of her breasts. His lips planted deep kisses into the lush fullness and tugged on the nipples, which pearled against his tongue.

She whimpered and clasped his head. "I love you too. I do. I didn't want to, but I do."

Their mouths came together hungrily. She had never known a feeling like that of his bare damp chest against her breasts. Mindlessly she rubbed herself against him and that electrifying carpet of hair.

There ensued an orgy of kissing that was interspersed with incoherent love words and sighs of immense pleasure and groans of building need.

"Brin, darling, my towel . . ."

"Yes?"

"It fell off."

Her arms were linked tightly around his neck. Her face was buried in the hollow of his shoulder and she could feel the warm pressure of his sex against her middle. "It did?" she asked in a small voice.

"Um-hm." He put enough space between them to

look down into her face, waiting until she raised her eyes to meet his. Then he lifted one of her hands from around his neck and kissed the palm fervently, sending a trill of sensation spearing pleasurably into her belly.

Slowly he carried her hand down. "Touch me."

He placed her hand in the general vicinity, but left the choice up to her. She could have refused, and he would have let her. But she loved him, and at that moment nothing seemed so important as demonstrating that love.

She flattened her hand on his abdomen. Slid it down. Her fingers sifted through the coarse hair, then encountered the velvety tip of his sex. Shyly she investigated it. With a sharp intake of breath he let his head fall forward onto her shoulder, and his whole body shuddered. He moaned audibly when she took him in a small, tight, gentle fist.

"Oh, my God . . . Brin . . . Sweet . . . I want . . . Ahh . . ." He kissed her with unleashed passion. Then he pressed his lips against her forehead and repeated again and again, "Be my lover. Be my lover. Be my . . ."

# *Five*

". . . lover."

It wasn't an echo from the past, but a heartfelt plea in the present. He held her tight. His lips moved against her cheek. "Be my lover, Brin. Be my wife again."

The doorbell pealed.

As though wrenched from a dream, Brin jumped away from him. Her face was flushed, her eyes glazed. The doorbell's chime had acted like a dash of cold water on her mounting desire. It had brought her to her senses, but she didn't know whether she was thankful for or resentful of the intrusion.

She turned and rushed into the living room. Riley was right behind her. She opened the door, sheltering her body behind it. "Abel?"

Brin hoped the man outside the door couldn't

hear Riley's muttered litany of profanity. She could imagine the way his brow was beetled with fury, but she dared not glance at him and give away his presence in the house. It might be difficult to explain. Her voice was as shaky as the hand she combed through her tangled hair. "This is certainly a surprise." That line was straight out of a B-movie script, but she hoped Riley believed it.

Riley could only hear Brin's half of the conversation. Standing ramrod-straight, his muscles rigid with rage, he strained to catch every word.

"No, I wasn't sleeping. . . . I would invite you in, but it's awfully late. . . . Of course I'm thinking about it, but I haven't reached a decision yet. . . . I said I'd tell you in the morning. That's what we agreed on. . . . I know, but please give me time. . . . Yes, I promise to tell you then. Good night." Quietly, as though she were afraid of rousing a potentially dangerous beast, she closed the door.

But the beast was already roused, as she found out when she turned to face Riley after Abel's car had driven off.

"Is it his habit to come courting after midnight?"

"No. And he didn't come courting."

"I'd like to know what the hell you call it."

"Nothing."

"How often does he do this 'nothing'?"

"Never. Tonight is the first night he's been here."

"You expect me to believe that?"

"It's the truth!"

"Why tonight?"

"He wanted to say thanks for the party again." Riley muttered something under his breath, and Brin was glad she hadn't caught all of it. The few key words she had heard were graphic enough. "He wanted to know if I had reached a decision about the job yet." She headed back toward the kitchen. Riley tracked her like a trained hunter. He was through the swinging door before it had time to close behind her.

"He said morning, didn't he? Well, didn't he? Wasn't that your deadline? Why is he badgering you about it tonight? Huh?" He was furious, and Brin knew his temper was something to dread. "I don't know where this guy gets off, even being as rich and powerful as he is, coming on to *my wife!*"

Riley slammed his hand down on the counter top. He didn't see the glass, didn't hear the crunching, splintering sound of it when it broke, didn't even feel the pain until Brin covered her mouth to stifle a scream. Puzzled, he looked down to see that the meaty part of his hand just beneath his thumb was pumping blood.

"Well, I'll be damned," he said softly.

Brin, petrified at first, sprang into action. She lunged for the sink and turned on the cold water. "Riley, oh, my God, does it hurt? Here, hold it over the sink, oh, Lord, it's bleeding, Riley." She blotted the wound with a dish towel, but her attempts at staunching the flow did no good. The red stain spread until the towel was soaked with it. "Oh, Riley," she said, sobbing. She crammed her own blood-stained fingers against her lips, and tears flooded her eyes.

Calmly Riley sponged the deep cut that ran from his thumb joint almost to his wrist. "I think I'll need a few stitches," he said with remarkable composure. "Will you drive me to the emergency room?"

"Yes, yes. Let's see. What . . ." She raised a hand to her forehead as though trying to arrange her darting thoughts into some semblance of order. The man she loved was bleeding profusely. She hadn't lived with him for seven months, but that thought never entered her mind. His pain was hers, and she would have laid down her own life at that moment to take away his hurt. "You'd better take your jacket." She swung the windbreaker over his shoulders. "Let me wrap up your hand with a clean towel."

She did so with fingers that operated automatically. If she had thought about the blood being Riley's, the torn flesh being his, she would have been totally ineffectual. "There, maybe that'll stop the bleeding until we get to the hospital. Where are my keys? Oh, here they are," she said, reaching for the hook by the back door where she always left her car keys.

"Careful, darling," she said, leading him down the back steps as though his legs were injured, and not his hand. "No, no, let me get the door for you. Are you in pain?"

"No," he lied with a brave smile.

"Don't lie to me, Riley! You are too. Your lips are white. I always know when you're in pain because your lips turn white. Remember that time you hurt your back playing softball? I knew you were in agony even though you swore you weren't."

She tucked him into the passenger's side and buckled the seat belt around him. Within seconds the Datsun was tearing through the hilly streets of San Francisco toward the nearest emergency clinic.

"Maybe you should elevate your hand just a little,

darling. There, isn't that better? Why don't you lay your head back? I'll have you there in no time."

"You'll make a terrific mommy."

"What?" She whipped her eyes off the road for only a fraction of a second. The speed at which she was driving wouldn't permit more than a momentary distraction. "A mommy?" she asked in a high, light voice.

"Yeah. I think we should have a couple of kids, don't you?"

"Well, I . . . I haven't thought about it lately."

"I have. They'd be terrific."

"Children are a big responsibility."

"Don't get me wrong. You wouldn't have to give up anything to have my baby. Selfishly, I'd want you to work producing my show for as long as you wanted to."

"I wouldn't want just one baby. I was an only child. You were too. You know that wasn't much fun. I'd want to have at least two."

"Then you agree that we should start a family?"

"Can't we talk about this later?" she asked absently. Blood was seeping through the towel wrapped around his hand. She touched his thigh in that unconscious, comfort-giving way a woman has with her man. "We're almost there."

She turned the car under the porte cochere of the emergency clinic and parked illegally. A policeman came up to her just as she was opening the door for Riley.

"Sorry, miss, but you can't leave your car here."

With a hand under Riley's right arm, she helped him alight and then turned to face the policeman. Since she had been married to Jon Riley, Brin had made it a cardinal rule not to use his name to secure the best tables in restaurants, or to obtain theater tickets when none were left to be obtained, or to demand special attention from anyone. Now, without even thinking about it, she broke that rule.

"This is Jon Riley. I'm his wife. He has hurt his hand and it's bleeding badly. I'm taking him in."

The policeman looked at Riley. "Well, whadayaknow! It *is* you! Me and the little woman wouldn't miss your show. I work nights, ya see, so I'm home in the daytime. It just wouldn't be morning without Riley. That's what we say."

"Could we just . . .?" Brin edged around him, nudging Riley forward.

"Sure, sure. Get him right on in there, miss, I mean Mrs. Riley. If you'll give me your keys, I'll park your car."

"They're in the ignition," she said over her shoulder.

She felt Riley shaking and glanced up worriedly, afraid he was about to faint from blood loss. The grin on his face revealed that his tremors came from laughter, not light-headedness. "Didn't you always say you'd never act like a star's wife? That you'd never throw my name up to people?"

"This is an emergency," she said primly.

His burst of laughter drew attention to them. As soon as the admitting nurse recognized him, she hustled them into an examination room, where they were immediately joined by a team of nurses. One unwrapped his hand and began to wash out the deep cut with a vigor that made Brin's stomach roil. One stuck a thermometer in his mouth. Another took his blood pressure. Brin, feeling useless all of a sudden, stood in the background.

The doctor strode in, saying, "I hear we have a celebrity in our midst."

"You'll forgive me for not shaking hands," Riley said with a wry grin as he extended his right hand for the doctor's inspection.

The doctor's vocal assessment of the wound was a series of grunts and "hmms" that had Brin shifting impatiently from one foot to the other while gnawing the inside of her cheek. Had the glass severed an artery? Was the muscle affected?

"It'll require some stitches. Should hurt like hell for a few days, but it'll be all right in a week or so." The doctor slapped Riley on the shoulder. "I'm gonna drink a cup of coffee while the nurse anesthetizes it and—"

"A shot?" Riley asked, paling for the first time.

"Several, I'm afraid."

"In my hand?" His voice quavered.

Brin pushed her way through the crowd of nurses, most of whom were sightseers. Riley reached for her. "He doesn't like shots. Needles."

"He'll like them even less if I sew up his hand without deadening it."

She put her arms around Riley's shoulders and held him close, smoothing the hair off his now-damp, pasty-gray forehead. "It'll be over soon, darling. I'll stay with you."

And she did, through it all, through the five deadening injections in his hand that coaxed sweat from every pore in his body, through the seventeen stitches, through the careful bandaging. She shushed him when he cursed, quipped jokes about hunks with no guts when he blanched at the sight of the syringe, and hugged him fiercely when the needle pierced the flesh around the angry cut.

The obliging policeman insisted on bringing her car up to the door as they left the building. Once on their way, Brin didn't have to suggest that Riley rest his head on the back of the seat. The effects of the accident were beginning to tell on him.

"I'm not really afraid of needles," he said drowsily, rolling his head to one side to watch her as she drove.

"You big liar. I remember when you had strep throat and had to get a shot of penicillin. The nurse you terrorized had to fetch me out of the waiting room before you'd cooperate and drop your pants."

"I think she only wanted a glimpse of Jon Riley's buns."

"As I recall, she wasn't impressed. I don't think anyone's buns would have impressed her. Try another lie."

"I only wanted a good excuse to pillow my head on your lovely breasts. And that's not a lie."

"You raised a ruckus that had us forever banned from that doctor's office just for that?"

"It was worth it. Just like tonight. Did you notice when I pecked a little kiss on the tip of one while no one was looking?"

She shot him a withering look. "Save it for someone who'll believe you, Riley. You're a crybaby."

"But did you notice?"

"Yes, yes, I noticed."

He chuckled at her exasperation and glanced out the windshield again. "Where are we going?"

"I'm taking you home."

"*My* home?"

"Yes," she said doubtfully. "What did you expect?"

"I expected you to let me spend the night at your place. This is my right hand, you know," he said, lifting the bandaged hand as though to remind her of it. "I could get a fever. I could go into shock. I could—"

"All right, all right, spare me the horror stories." She executed a U-turn at the next traffic light. "But don't read anything into this. I'm just doing what any compassionate human being would do for a fellow man."

"I understand. And don't think I don't appreciate it." He said it solemnly, but she sensed the amusement behind his words. They rode in silence for a few blocks, before he said, "Know what this reminds me of?"

"What?"

"The night we got married."

The car swerved and Brin swore. "Pothole," she said by way of explanation for her carelessness.

But Riley knew she was thinking about the night she had become his wife. "We just dropped everything and set off for Lake Tahoe. Remember?"

How could she ever forget? "You dropped everything, literally."

"My towel?"

"Yes."

"Lord," he groaned as his memory carried him back. "Your hand was on me and I was dying. I said, 'Be my lover, Brin.' And you said . . ."


"No, Riley. I can't." She pushed herself away from him. She cast her eyes down, then quickly up again. Oh, he was beautiful.

"Can't?" he rasped.

"Won't."

"You said you love me."

"I do," she moaned. "I do. But I won't be just another of your groupies. I know about all the scalps dangling from your belt. Your sexual exploits are a favorite topic of conversation around the coffee machine at work. I don't want my name to be bandied about with all the others. And when you got tired of me and broke off the affair, we could never work together again."

"You're saying you won't go to bed with me?"

"That's right."

Gently he laid his hands on her shoulders. "You don't believe me when I say I love you?"

"I believe you believe it. But—"

"You don't think what I feel for you is different? That it's something permanent?"

She caught her lower lip between her teeth and shook her head.

"I do love you, Brin. And I want to make love to you. What do I have to do to get you into bed with me?"

Her answer was flippant. "Marry me."

"All right."

She almost dislocated several vertebrae in her neck when her head snapped up. "*What?*"

"I said, 'All right.' I'll marry you. I was hoping that would be your condition. It saved me from going down on bended knee. Do you realize how ridiculous a naked man looks on bended knee? And what if you said no? There I'd be, naked to the world and humiliated all at the same time."

"B—but I was only joking."

His brow arched over his frowning eyes in the way that made the women in his audience swoon.

"Do you always play with a man like this, joke about marriage?"

"No, but—"

"Will you marry me, Brin?"

She got lost in the deep, cerulean pools of his eyes, and never quite remembered saying yes.

"This is crazy," she said a half hour later as they sped toward the Sierras and Lake Tahoe.

"I'm crazy about you. Crazy, and in love for the first time in my life." His free hand was taking liberties at the front of her dress.

"We're going to be the two craziest people ever sealed in caskets if you don't keep your eyes on the road and . . . uh, your hands on the wheel."

"Want me to stop?" he drawled close to her ear as his fingers lightly brushed her nipple.

"Hmm, no." Her hand crept higher up his thigh. She squeezed him gently.

He cursed softly and removed his hand from her bodice. "Fair's fair, and you've made your point."

She settled back in the car seat and said dreamily, "My folks will be so disappointed. Mother always wanted me to have a church wedding, long white dress, the works. She's wasted a lot of money by subscribing to *Bride* all these years."

"We'll call them tomorrow morning and invite them to fly up for the rest of the weekend. Separate suites, of course," he added. "Will they like me?"

"Only a few weeks ago Mother *very casually* remarked that I should settle down and marry a 'nice young man like that Jon Riley.' That I should have a family, a house with a yard and a dog, and stop concentrating on a career."

"And your father?" There was a trace of uncertainty in his voice. Brin had talked about her father and his stern, military bearing. "What does the admiral think about me?"

"He grunted something about your hair being too long. But then, he thinks everyone's hair is too long. If that's his only criticism, you're in like Flynn. What about your mother?" She knew that Riley's father was deceased, but that his mother lived in San Jose.

"I'll call and invite her up too. We'll turn it into a real family affair and try to make amends for not inviting them to the wedding."

"But will your mother like me?"

"Are you kidding?" he asked, turning his head to look at her. "She thinks I'm a smart aleck and has been telling me for years that what I needed was a good woman who would take me to task."

Brin laughed and snuggled against him. "I just want to take you."

During the long drive they exchanged bits and pieces of themselves, filling in the years they hadn't known each other, getting acquainted as lovers do.

Brin had expected to be married in one of the tacky wedding chapels that sprouted up like weeds along the highway the moment they crossed the state line into Nevada. Invariably these chapels had gawdy neon lights that boasted low rates, advertised the fact that no blood tests were required, and bragged that they were open twenty-four hours a day. Organ music and artificial flowers were available at extra cost.

But Riley braked the car in front of a quaint church nestled in a grove of pine trees. It had a steeple and stained-glass windows with a glowing, mellow light shining through them. He assisted

Brin out of his low, sleek sports car and guided her up the steps and through the arched front door of the church.

Brin gasped with pleasure and surprise when she stepped inside. The entire chapel was lit with candles and decorated with flowers, real ones, all white. At the head of the carpeted center aisle, in front of the altar, stood a bespectacled minister who looked like he'd stepped out of a Norman Rockwell painting. A buxom woman, probably his wife, was smiling angelically from her place at the organ, which filled the chapel with traditional wedding music.

"You don't happen to be Catholic or Jewish, do you?" Riley asked with a concerned frown.

"No."

"So a Protestant service is okay?"

"Yes, it's . . ." She choked up. "When did you arrange this?"

"I called from your apartment when you went in the bedroom to change and pack. Are you pleased?"

"Pleased?" she asked with a soft smile, reaching up to touch his cheek. "You are so dear. I love you."

"I love you too," he said huskily, bending to kiss her fervently. Moments later the minister tactfully cleared his throat to break them apart.

After the meaningful exchange of vows, Riley drove Brin to a resort hotel at the base of one of the ski lifts. "I've never been here, but I understand it's five-star-rated."

As well it should be, they noted the moment they entered. An elevator swept them up from the lavish, antique-furnished lobby, complete with a grand piano and an enormous fireplace, to a suite that made Brin gape like a girl straight out of the sticks. There was a small kitchenette and wet bar between the sitting room and bedroom. A redwood hot tub gurgled in one corner of the bathroom. A fireplace was situated in the bedroom opposite the king-sized bed.

"Ready to cut your wedding cake?" Riley asked as she surveyed the suite, taking in every well-thought-out convenience and luxury.

"Wedding cake?"

The cart that the deferential waiter wheeled into the sitting room contained, not a cake, but a souf-flé, rising a good two inches above its white baking dish and looking as fluffy and light as a giant marshmallow. It was nestled in a stiff linen napkin folded to represent a swan. The "swan" was swimming through a pond of white flower petals. Brin surveyed the epicurean artwork through tear-blurred eyes and only prayed that, if this were all a dream, it would last till morning.

"It's lovely."

After checking with Riley to see if they would be needing anything else, the waiter withdrew. Riley divided the rich vanilla soufflé, smothered Brin's portion with creamy Grand Marnier sauce, and served it to her. They fed each other bites, licking each other's fingers when they got wonderfully messy.

Champagne followed. Feeling as bubbly and golden as the wine, Brin let Riley lead her from the sitting room into the bedroom. Taking her cham-pagne glass from her, he set it aside and faced his bride. His hot blue gaze rained down on her face. "Well, here we are," he said softly. . . .

* * *

"Here we are." Brin braked the car in her garage and pushed the button to close the door behind them. "Were you asleep?" she asked as Riley lifted his head and blinked his eyes open.

"No. Just thinking about our wedding night."

She had been thinking about the same thing, but she wouldn't allow herself to enter into a conversation about it. Not now. Not when Riley's eyes were darkly ringed with fatigue and his face looked gaunt and pale from loss of blood. Not when she was feeling maternal and caring and protective toward him. Not when he was spending the night with her.

She ushered him inside, cautioning him to avoid stepping on the broken glass that had showered the kitchen floor. "Would you like anything?" she asked as she lifted his jacket off his shoulders. "To eat? To drink?"

He shook his head, and without another word she led him upstairs to the bedroom. "Does your hand hurt?" she asked sympathetically as she flung back the covers on the bed.

"No, it's numb. It would be my right hand, wouldn't it? It probably won't be much use to me for the next few days."

"You'll have to take it easy. You lost a lot of blood."

"I'm just glad I didn't need a transfusion. I'm not sure I could stand having a needle in my arm that long." He slipped out of his shoes and dropped to the edge of the bed to peel off his socks. When he automatically lifted his right hand to unbutton his shirt, he realized just how incapacitated he was.

"Here, let me." Brin hurried to his aid. Taking

his arm, she pulled him to his feet. He stood before her, his arms hanging loosely at his sides. With deft fingers she unbuttoned the first few buttons. It was only when the backs of her knuckles brushed against the soft, springy hair on his chest that her movements became clumsy.

Suddenly she became aware of just how intimate the procedure of undressing him was going to be. A reflection of days gone by. Of nights when they had made a deliciously naughty game of undressing each other. Or, in a sweet rush of passion, had nearly ripped the clothes from each other's bodies.

She pulled the shirttail from the waistband of his jeans and exposed his chest. It was so achingly familiar, as familiar to her as her own face in the mirror. The dark forest of hair, the taut, tanned skin, the flat coppery nipples, which she knew responded to the merest touch of fingertips or tongue. He was lean enough that every rib was visible. His stomach was flat and corrugated with muscle, his navel deep and hair-whorled.

As casually as possible, she tossed his shirt across the chair. "Do you, uh, want your jeans off?"

"I don't usually sleep in them."

Her head was bowed. She wondered if he knew she was feeling dizzy and breathless. To ward off the vertigo, she closed her eyes until she was able to continue. Her hands had to be forced to move to his belt. The metal buckle was cool against her fingers, but the skin beneath the snap was warm as she fumbled to open it.

She pulled the zipper down slowly, stretching the cloth as far away from his body as it would go. Which wasn't far, since he wore his jeans as snug as decency would allow. It was impossible to pretend that the firm evidence of his sex didn't exist or that she couldn't feel it against the backs of her fingers.

When the zipper was all the way down, she slid her hands into the waistband of the jeans at the sides of his hips and eased them down over hard, trim thighs. She went down on her knees in front of him and drew the pants past sinewy calves until he was able to step out of them.

"I don't usually sleep in my underwear, either," he said thickly.

She tilted her head far back, gazing up the entire length of his body to meet his eyes. His rawly masculine image seemed to sway in front of her like an erotic mirage. She wanted nothing more than to rest her cheek against the strong columns of his thighs, to hug his hard frame against her. To kiss the hair-roughened skin. To taste—

Realizing where her thoughts were taking her, she surged to her feet. "Well, you'll have to suffer tonight." She virtually shoved him down on the bed. As soon as his head hit the pillow, she raised the sheet and blanket over him as though she couldn't bear to look at him a moment longer. And it wasn't because he repulsed her.

The bathroom door slammed behind her as she retreated like a cowardly soldier seeking respite from the battleground. She stripped for the second time that night and pulled on a cotton knit panty and tank top. She loved sleeping in them for their form-fitting comfort. They were a designer's copy of masculine underwear, but the way Brin's figure filled them out left no doubt as to her gender. Over the matched set, which was robin's-egg blue, she pulled on an old robe that Riley had once claimed worked better than a headache as a turn-off.

Switching off the light, she reentered the bedroom. "Do you need anything?"

He had lowered the covers to his waist. His left arm was folded beneath his head. His bandaged right hand was resting on his lap. "Only some tender, loving care. I'd like to continue our discussion about having babies. You know, Brin, living apart as we are is going to make it damn hard to make . . . What are you doing?"

"Getting down covers," she answered from the closet.

"What for?"

"For the bed I'm going to make on the couch downstairs."

He sprang to a sitting position, obviously annoyed. "Oh, for heaven's sake, Brin."

"No, for *my* sake and yours. We can't muddy up this issue any more than it already is by sleeping together tonight. I hope that's not what you had in mind when you asked to spend the night here." His glowering frown made it clear that that was exactly what he'd had in mind. "Good night, Riley. I'll see you in the morning." With all the imperiousness of a queen, she swept out of the bedroom, trailing the end of a blanket behind her like a royal train.

She heard his terse expletive and smiled to herself.

But the joke was on her. Even though the sofa was long enough to accommodate her and as comfortable as any bed, she couldn't sleep. Damn him for reminding her of their wedding night!

It had been as enchanting as a fairy tale. Romantic. Sexy. And as she tossed and turned on the sofa, her thoughts seemed bent on returning to it. . . .

"Well, here we are," he said softly. The ivory satin sheets beckoned them from the bed. A fire was burning in the gas fireplace for effect. Its flickering light projected their shadows on the walls and was reflected in their eyes. "Would you like to try out the hot tub?"

"Maybe afterward."

"Afterward?" he asked, raising his brows teasingly.

Her cheeks grew pink. "Later," she amended.

"Does that mean you want to get in bed as fast as I do?"

"Yes, please," she said politely. "Besides, it's nearly dawn." She laid her hand on the placket of his shirt. "If we don't hurry, we won't have a wedding *night*."

"We sure as hell can't let that happen, can we?" He nuzzled her throat, his arms sliding around her waist. "Would you like a few minutes alone?"

"Not necessarily," she breathed against his neck.

"Then, do I have permission to undress you?" He waited for her answer, and when none was forthcoming, he raised his head and looked down at her. Her eyes were smoky with desire, her lips moist and inviting. She nodded her head and stepped out of her shoes, taking several inches off her height and making her seem more feminine than she already did.

The jacquard silk dress was monochromatic tones of white. One shoulder had a row of pearl buttons, which Riley dexterously unfastened. He reached beneath her left arm to slide down the side zipper. The dress shimmied down her body. She was left standing in a champagne-colored slip that robbed Riley of breath. Her breasts amply filled the stretchy lace cups, making a brassiere unnecessary.

He slipped his thumbs beneath the satin straps and eased them off her shoulders. "I don't know whether to kiss you or look at you," he murmured.

"Why not both?"

After a kiss that left them dazed, his eyes drifted over her lazily. She held her breath as he lowered the slip to her waist. Her breasts held his eyes captive for a long time. Then, with the same blend of tenderness and passion that he had demonstrated before, he cupped her breasts in his hands and made love to them with his mouth.

"Riley." She sighed and clasped handfuls of his hair between her fingers as his tongue played upon her with undivided attention and nimble expertise.

He lowered his head farther and kissed her stomach, then sank to his knees and pressed his face into the softness of her belly. Her slip was removed by unhurried hands. He gazed at the pale stockings and lacy garter belt with a mixture of excitement and impatience.

He carefully unhooked the garters and rolled the stockings down her legs, taking precious time to measure the fit of her calves in his palms. When the veil-sheer stockings had been removed, he slid his hands up and down the backs of her legs from derriere to ankles. She shivered and made faint mewling sounds that brought a smile of pure male arrogance to his lips. He unfastened the garter belt, and it dropped from her hips.

The sheer panties hid nothing. His eyes moved over her rapaciously. But when he removed that last airy garment, he reined in his passion and savored her nakedness with an attitude of worship.

He enfolded her in his arms. Pressing his fingers into the fullness of her buttocks, he drew her close. He feathered light kisses across her abdomen, leaving the skin damp with caresses. Finally his lips melted into the soft dark cloud of hair. He used his tongue to express his joy in her.

Brin uttered a soft cry as her knees gave way and thumped against his chest. She would have collapsed had he not stood, caught her against him, and carried her to the bed. Before she had opened her eyes fully, he was naked, too, and lowering himself over her. She welcomed him, pulling him close, arching against him as their mouths came together.

He tested her preparedness with loving fingers that parted and stroked until she was moving restlessly, her legs sawing wantonly against his. Sensations swirled through her lower body. The flower of her sex bloomed open, and she ached for his possession. Then he was there, warm and hard and full. Sliding into her. Uniting them.

He raised his head in surprise and started to ease away. Brin wouldn't let him; she tightened her limbs around him. "I love you, Riley," she whispered, her lips moving against his nipple. "I love you."

It took a long, lusty time, but his body patiently rocked hers to fulfillment. He nestled inside her after he was spent, reluctant to leave the small, tight warmth she gloved him in. Dawn crept through the draperies, bathing their sweat-dampened bodies with rosy light. "My sweet, sweet bride," he said in a voice that told her she was cherished. He kissed her ear, her neck, her mouth, her breasts. "I love you, Brin."

"I love you, Jon."

Lifting his head, he looked down into slumberous aquamarine eyes. "That's the first time you've called me that. Sure you've got the right guy?"

She smiled sleepily and drew his head back down to her breasts. "I've got the right guy. Jon, Jon, Jon . . ."

Brin shifted uncomfortably on the sofa. Sleep stubbornly eluded her. When she heard a noise on the stairs, she sat up abruptly and spoke aloud the name that had been echoing through the chambers of her mind for hours. "Jon?"

# *Six*

---

Brin switched on the lamp. Riley, who was groping his way downstairs, was blinded by the sudden light, and blinked against it. "What did you say?"

"What? When? What are you doing out of bed?" She flung off the covers and rushed to the foot of the stairs, thinking he might need assistance.

"You called me Jon."

"Did I?"

"Yes. You never call me Jon except when we're making love."

"I must have been dreaming."

"Must have been a helluva dream."

His insinuating smile poured over her like warm honey. Her body's tingling response to it vexed her. "You haven't said what you're doing out of bed."

"You didn't ask."

"I did so."

"You did? Hmm. I must have been shell-shocked by hearing you call me Jon."

He took the remaining stairs and came to stand above her on the last step. Only then did Brin fully realize that he was as scantily dressed as she. He was wearing nothing more than what she'd last seen him in, a pair of cotton briefs . . . *brief* cotton briefs, which rode low on his narrow hips. She loved that spot, an inch or two beneath his navel, where the satiny stripe of hair began to unfurl. He loved being kissed there too. Loved—

She jerked her eyes up to his face and caught his mocking smile. Uncomfortably aware of the brevity of her costume, she crossed her arms over her chest. The ugly robe had been left behind in her hurry, leaving her in nothing more than the bikini panty and tank top, which clung like a second skin.

"You've got great legs," Riley whispered roughly.

Months ago, when they had lived together as husband and wife, neither of them had exhibited a trace of modesty. Nakedness had never been awkward. Now, with the stillness of the night closing around them, with the specter of their separation looming between them, with his intense blue eyes boring into her, Brin felt more naked than ever in her life. Exposed. Vulnerable.

Any small animal whose weaknesses have been exploited will lash out at its predator. In this case, Brin's only weapon was hostility. "You came all the way downstairs, woke me up, to tell me that?"

"No, but as long as I was here . . ." He shrugged. "The anesthetic is wearing off."

Her animosity vanished and her brow puckered with concern. "Your hand hurts?"

"Like hell."

"The doctor said it would when the deadening began wearing off. He gave me some pain pills for you to take. They're in my purse in the kitchen. I'll get them."

She turned in that direction, but Riley grasped her wrist and stopped her. "I don't want a pain pill."

"But if it hurts—"

"I'd rather have a brandy. That'll numb the pain, but won't knock me out. Join me in one?"

With his fingers still loosely clasped around her wrist, he pulled her across the room to the bar. She padded after him docilely. The lateness of the hour lent a surrealistic quality to the occasion. Were they actually walking around in the middle of the night, in her friend's extravagantly decorated living room, in their underwear? It seemed impossible, yet it was so.

He deposited her on a stool and circled the end of the bar. His search through the stock turned up, not one, but two, brands of brandy. He selected the more expensive and poured a hefty portion into a snifter.

"None for me, thanks," Brin said, curling her toes over the rung of the stool.

"A liqueur? Bailey's? I know you love Bailey's."

"Nothing."

"Then, cheers." He tipped the snifter toward her before taking a sip. He closed his eyes as the burning liquor slid down his throat, through his chest, and into his stomach, where it spread its welcome fire through his belly. There was a taut white line outlining his lips. His nostrils were pinched.

Brin touched the bandaged hand. "It really does hurt, doesn't it?"

"I'm all right," he said with that air of masculine superiority over pain that drives women to distraction.

"Why can't you just admit that it hurts?"

"Why whine about it?"

"Because when someone doesn't feel good he's entitled to a little sympathy, that's why. It's natural and normal."

"Does that apply to women too?"

"Certainly."

He started laughing.

"What's funny?" she asked.

"Is that why you always went to bed when you got cramps?"

"Cramps hurt," she said defensively. "If you had had to suffer them a single day of your life, you would have carried on something terrible. Any man would."

He reached out and put his palm against her cheek. "I know they hurt." His thumb stroked her lower lip. "But we discovered a no-fail cure for them, didn't we?"

Brin swallowed hard. She lowered her eyes. She shifted restlessly on the stool.

"And our method beat Midol all to hell," he added raspily.

"I don't remember."

"Yes, you do."

"How do you know what I remember?" she challenged.

His eyes slid down her throat to her chest. She followed his gaze down, but she already knew what had given her away. She could feel her nipples straining against their soft confinement.

"Take your brandy upstairs," she said quickly, sliding off the stool. "I'm going back to bed."

She returned to the couch and made a production of fluffing up her pillow. It didn't need it, but the activity gave her something to do so she wouldn't see the knowing look in his eyes.

She lay down and pulled the blanket over her shoulders, turning on her side and pretending that sleep was imminent. She felt the sofa sag with his weight as he sat down on the end opposite her head. He lifted her feet into his lap. With an annoyed sigh she rolled over and looked at him.

"You said you were taking your brandy upstairs."

"No, *you* said I was taking my brandy upstairs. You're sure having a hard time keeping straight who says what tonight. Could it be that you're flustered because I'm here?"

She made a scoffing sound and closed her eyes in feigned boredom. "All right, stay. I don't care. Only be quiet so I can sleep." She sighed deeply and closed her eyes again. But seconds later she jackknifed into a sitting position. "And stop that!"

"You always did have sensitive feet." His left hand was beneath the covers. His thumb had gone straight for the spot where the ball of her foot met her big toe. A mere touch, much less a rotating massage of his thumb, had always elicited a reaction from her.

"You're not going to let me sleep, are you?" she demanded.

"How can you sleep when I'm suffering?"

"The brandy's not helping?"

"Not yet." He held up the snifter. He hadn't drunk but a third of it.

"All right," Brin said tiredly. "I'll baby-sit you. But if you become drunk and rowdy instead of sedated, I'm packing you off home. You can drive with your left hand."

"You should know," he said with a lazy grin.

Heat surged through her as she recalled all the times he had done just that while his right hand was otherwise occupied. She rebelled at her own tendency to remember the past; she certainly didn't need his less-than-subtle reminders of it. "Stop making lewd insinuations, or I'll send you upstairs."

"I was surprised to discover you were a virgin on our wedding night."

"Riley! Didn't you hear what I just said?"

"That wasn't an insinuation. That was a simple statement of fact. I was surprised."

"Why?"

"There aren't many virgins your age left."

"My age? You make me sound ancient. Like a relic from the past."

"How old were you? Twenty-five? Come on, Brin. How many twenty-five-year-old virgins do you know?"

"Maybe they should all be rounded up and herded into museums."

"You sound piqued. I only said I was surprised. I didn't say I was disappointed." He was stroking the high arch of her foot with an indolent thumb. "In fact I liked it very much," he said softly. "It would have driven me crazy if I had had to imagine who'd been with you before me. I couldn't have stood the thought of other men making love to you."

The unrelenting caress on her feet was lulling her into a trance. She was remembering all the times his tongue had performed that same ritual, turning her bones to butter and her blood to simmering, liquid desire. That he still had that hypnotizing effect on her was something she resented. Unwisely she spoke aloud the first retort that flashed into her mind.

"There are other ways of making love."

His thumb came to an abrupt standstill. Brin felt the angry tension in his fingers as they closed more tightly around her foot. She watched his dark brows pull into a harsh V above his nose. "What's that supposed to mean?"

She wished for all the world that she hadn't opened her mouth, that she had weighed his reaction to such an oblique boast before speaking aloud. But there was no backing down now. "Just that I never said other men hadn't made love to me. Because my virginity was intact you assumed as much."

"Meaning you played around a lot, you just never went 'all the way'?"

She shrugged.

"With whom?"

"Oh, honestly, Riley. What difference does—"

"I'll tell you what difference it makes. It makes a helluva lot of difference to me, that's what difference it makes."

"Why? Why now? It didn't matter when we were married."

"When we were married you didn't flaunt your former lovers in my face."

"I didn't flau—"

"Who were they? Men you knew in college?"

He was making her mad. His stupidity and obstinacy were fanning her smoldering anger into a wildfire. "Of course. I went to Berkeley, you know."

"Oh, of course. That explains a lot." His eyes narrowed to fine blue slits. "High school?"

"Some," she said with a toss of her head.

"Junior high?" When she only glared back at him defiantly, he whispered, "My God." His eyes raked down her body as though seeing it for the first time. "Did you lead all those men a merry chase the way you did me before we married? Tease them until they were nearly crazy? How far did you let the poor bastards go?"

"This is ridiculous."

"*How far?*" he shouted. "Did you let them see your breasts? Touch them?"

"I won't—"

"Kiss them? What about your thighs?"

"Riley—"

"Did they kiss your thighs? Between them?"

"Stop this! I won't listen to any more!"

She tried to extricate her feet from his grasp, but his left hand seemed to have assumed the strength of two. He imprisoned her ankles in an iron grip and firmly tucked her heels into the notch of his lap. "Oh, yes, you will. You'll listen to it all. You brought this up, now I want to thoroughly exhaust the subject."

"There *is* no subject. There were no men."

"Did you love them back? With your hands, your mouth? How did they love you?"

"They didn't! *There were no other men!*" Her shout finally penetrated the red mist of jealous rage that fogged his brain.

His bare chest was heaving with each ragged

breath. She saw him visibly pull himself together, though he didn't release his hold on her feet. "Who was your first lover? Who?"

"You were." She strained the two words between her teeth. Her whole body was vibrating with humiliation and fury.

For several ponderous moments they stared at each other, then Brin flopped back onto the pillow. Wearily she raised one forearm over her eyes. "There. Is that what you wanted to hear?"

"You hadn't ever—"

"No, Riley, I hadn't ever." She lowered her arm and looked at him. Both of them were surprised by the tears forming in her eyes. "Couldn't you tell? Didn't you know? Is your ego so fragile that you had to have me spell it out for you?"

He laid his injured hand in the valley at the center of her rib cage and, with the slightest movement of his fingers, stroked her tummy. "Why did you say there had been other men?"

"To provoke you, I guess," she admitted listlessly.

"Why did you want to provoke me?"

"I don't know. Maybe because of the other women." The tears were dried now. Her eyes were as deep and turbulent as the bay during a Pacific storm. "The women before *and* after we were married. You've been going out. I read the newspapers."

His hand became still, then was completely withdrawn. He reached for the brandy, which he had set on the end table, and took a long sip. When he returned the snifter to the table he said curtly, "You've been out too. Winn's been squiring you around for weeks."

"How do you know that?"

"I have my sources."

"I've explained Abel to you. There's nothing romantic about our friendship."

"The same is true when a woman accompanies me on a personal appearance."

She looked at him skeptically. His face drew into a self-righteous frown. "You know what those social events are like. I'm expected to attend them on behalf of the TV station. I'm also expected to have an escort. Those dates don't mean anything. Nothing happens."

"I know better," she said, springing to a sitting position again. "I remember the time we went—" She broke off in mid-sentence. "Never mind."

His mouth tilted up at the corner. "Come on. Finish. You remember what time?"

"Nothing. I forgot."

"Could you be referring to the night I spoke at that Marin County shindig? The night they sent the limousine for us?"

The fiery blush that spread across Brin's cheeks was as good as a signed confession. . . .


"How did we rate this?" Brin asked.

The limousine that had come for them at the appointed time was long, black, and luxurious. The chauffeur seemed to sit at least half a block away from the back seat, where Brin rode with Riley.

"You rate it because you're with me. And I rate it because I'm a famous television personality."

"And such a humble, self-effacing one," she said

with amusement and affection. Leaning forward, she kissed him on the cheek.

"Hey, look at this," he exclaimed with boyish enthusiasm as he discovered the button that operated the electric moon roof. "And there's a stocked bar, lest madam get thirsty." He showed her the panel that slid open to reveal the bar. "And there's a color TV in case you don't want to miss an episode of *Dallas*."

He played with all the gadgets and buttons. "Just don't break anything," she cautioned. "We couldn't afford to have it repaired."

"You're not to worry your pretty little head about this family's finances," he said in the chauvinistic manner he knew irritated her. He grinned when he got the expected baleful look. "My agent's just negotiated a new contract. It embarrasses me when I consider what they're paying me."

"I'll bet," she said dryly.

"And I've been informed by inside sources that my producer is up for a big raise too."

"Who told you that?"

"My wife. Who has an inside track with my producer."

"Just don't forget that one doesn't overlap the other. Your producer was recommended for a raise because of her brilliant handling of *Riley in the Morning* and the substantial increase in its rating points."

"And what reward does she get for her brilliant handling of Riley?" he growled close to her ear.

"Hmm, just more of Riley, I guess." She purred seductively and curved her hand around the back of his head as he leaned over to kiss her.

"Have I told you how delectable you look tonight? Is that a new blouse?"

"No and yes, in that order." Her lips sipped at his. "You look pretty tasty yourself, Mr. Riley. I happen to become wild and irresponsible where men in tuxedoes are concerned."

"I wish you'd told me that before." The conversation was momentarily suspended by a lengthy kiss. "Know what I just realized?"

"No, what?"

"That I haven't seen you all day."

"You saw me for hours at work."

"But that was work. And once we got home you were busy getting ready for tonight and put me to work planting those bedding plants on the patio."

"Did you miss me?"

"I missed this." He thrust his tongue deep inside her mouth and his arms closed more tightly around her.

When they finally pulled apart she murmured, "I'm flattered. We've been married ten whole months and you're not tired of me yet."

"Not a chance," he whispered against her neck. "In fact, if you'll lower your hand a few more inches, you'll see just how tired of you I ain't."

"Riley!" she said, giggling.

"Sorry. Just how tired of you I'm not."

"Shh! The driver will hear you."

Reaching behind him for the panel of buttons, he found the one that raised a partition to separate them from the chauffeur. "There. All taken care of. Ever made love in a limousine?"

"No, and . . . ah, darling . . . behave, now. The chauffeur . . . hmm . . ."

Unconsciously she slipped off her high-heeled

sandals and rubbed her stockinged foot against his calf. Her arms folded around his neck as he lowered her into the plush corner of the limousine, which received her like a velvet embrace.

"I really like this blouse." It was black, sheer organza, and the rhinestone buttons cooperated with his busy fingers. "I like the way it rustles. Ever notice how sexy the sound of rustling clothes is?" She wore a black lace teddy beneath the blouse.

"Riley, we really shouldn't." Her protest was weak because he was already massaging her breasts, lifting and reshaping them within his hands. "Three hundred people are waiting for you and . . . hmm . . . you'll forget what you're supposed to . . . to, uh, oh, Riley . . . say."

"I bet you taste as good as you look."

He slipped his hand inside the webby lace cup and lifted her breast free. His thumb finessed the crest into sweet arousal, then he lowered his head and took it between his lips. He worried the tender peak with his tongue, flicking crazily and stroking sinuously until Brin was almost delirious with pleasure. She blindly tore at the studs of his tuxedo shirt until his chest was bare and her hands could thrill to the feel of his skin, his chest hair.

The black moire skirt she was wearing to the formal affair crackled appealingly as his free hand slipped beneath it. The skin of her upper thigh was soft, silky, and his fingertips derived as much pleasure from their caress as they gave. His fingers tiptoed up the suspenders to the satin garter belt, then stroked the warm skin above it.

When his hand slipped inside the matching panties and cupped her femininity, they both gasped softly. "Jon, that's . . . oh, yes."

"You're so sweet. And wet. So wet. I love touching you like this. And like this."

His fingers explored. Deliciously. Her throat arched and her head ground into the velour upholstery. She bit her bottom lip to keep from crying out her ecstasy.

Her response enflamed him. He withdrew his hand and frantically opened the zipper of his trousers. His possession was swift. They were frenzied by the impropriety of what they were doing. The threat of discovery, the ruination of the fine clothing that was bunched between their straining bodies, only served to heighten their excitement. His hands opened wide over the fleshy part of her bottom and drew her up hard against him. His hips ground into her, rolling and thrusting madly.

The crisis came quickly, like an explosion that shuddered soundlessly through them simultaneously. He buried his face in her neck and released his groans of completion in a hot torrent of breath against her fevered skin. Replete, her arms fell away from his neck.

And just as simultaneously, they began laughing.

"Oh, my gosh, Riley. What have we done? You'd better get off me and let me assess the damage."

He raised his head and peered out the window— which was tinted, luckily. "You'd better hurry, sweetheart. I'd say we have three minutes at the outside."

"Oh, no," she squeaked. Her clothes were put in order swiftly enough, but one sandal couldn't be found until she got down on all fours on the floorboard and groped beneath the seat.

"I can't find one of my studs, Brin," Riley said in near panic. "Oh, here it is . . . no, that's part of the seat belt."

"Ouch, damn! Here it is. I just found the little devil with my heel. It's probably put a run in my stocking."

He inserted the stud, tucked his shirt in, and replaced the cummerbund. "Don't forget to zip up," Brin said.

"Thanks." His bow tie was crooked, and Brin took time out from recombing her hair to straighten it. Swift fingers reattached the decorative comb in her hair, and she checked her compact mirror for damage wreaked on her makeup, with which she had taken great pains.

Through the tinted windows they could see that a small welcoming committee was waiting to greet them beneath the awning of the exclusive country club. "How do I look?" Brin asked anxiously as the limousine glided to a halt.

"Like you've just made love."

"Riley!"

"Well, you asked." Laughing, he took her hand and squeezed it. "Look at it this way, all the women will be jealous of you and all the men will be jealous of me. I doubt many of them had a tumble on their way here."

She began laughing. "I love you."

"And I love you." His face grew almost fierce. "Swear to God I do."

The chauffeur came around to the back door of the limousine and opened it. Much to the amusement of their welcoming committee, Mr. and Mrs. Jon Riley were caught kissing. . . .

"Admit it," Riley said softly. "It was fun."

"I never said it wasn't fun." Brin was plucking at a loose thread on the blanket. "You were always fun." Her eyes drifted up to his, and she looked at him through a thick screen of lashes. "How much fun have you had with other women since I left? Taken any limousine rides lately?"

He gently lifted her feet off his lap and, taking up the brandy snifter, leaned forward and propped his elbows on his knees. He swirled the snifter with his left hand as he stared down into its contents.

"I was mad as hell when you left, Brin," he began quietly.

Suddenly Brin didn't want to know. Why had she provoked him into telling her? She didn't want to hear his confession. But it was too late. He had made up his mind to tell her.

"Without a word, you were just gone." He turned only his head, but it swiveled toward her so abruptly, she jumped, and recoiled from the laser action of his eyes. "Do you blame me for being hurt? What if I had just moved out on you without one word of explanation, recrimination, regret, remorse, anything?"

"I guess you had reason to be angry," she conceded softly.

"Damn right I did." He tossed down a draft of brandy. "Until I got your letter in the mail, I was crazy with worry."

"But I left you a note."

"Oh, sure. Five words. Big deal. 'Don't worry. I'll

be fine.' Don't worry, with perverts walking the streets. And there are plane crashes and car accidents happening every day." His agitation mounted with each word. "Lakes and oceans to drown in. Mountains to fall off. I thought of them all." He drew a deep breath, which calmed him. " 'Don't worry.' I swear, if I could have gotten my hands on you that night I would have strangled you!"

He shot off the couch and began to pace. "Then, when I got your letter, which instead of giving an explanation, only told me to stay away from you, I got mad. Fighting mad. Spitting mad. I wasn't too friendly a fellow to be around. Couldn't and wouldn't work. When the station manager called and told me either to shape up without you or get out for good, I regained my sanity. Why should I let you ruin my career, my life? So I went back to work. And that's when the indifference set in."

"That's when you started seeing other women," she said dully.

"Well, why not? How did I know you weren't dating? How did I know you hadn't been having an affair the whole time we were married?"

She gave him a dirty look and he relented. "All right, I never really thought that, but it crossed my mind. So I started dating. And the younger and sweeter and more obliging they were, the better I liked them."

She buried her chin in her chest. She wouldn't cry. She wouldn't! After all, what had she expected? Nobody had to tell her how potent Riley's sex drive was. He was sure to have sought an outlet for his frustration.

"Some women will do anything to make sure a

man asks them out again," he said tauntingly. "And at the risk of sounding boorishly conceited, I didn't have to go far to find the most cooperative ones."

Having stood all she could, Brin threw back the blanket and lunged off the couch. "I think I'll have a drink now." She strode toward the bar.

"There were plenty of women at my disposal, Brin."

"I have no doubt of that," she threw over her shoulder. "But spare me the salacious details. I don't need to hear any more." She slammed a highball glass onto the bar and held a bottle of Bailey's over it.

"But I didn't sleep with any of them."

Brin's hand froze in the act of pouring the cream liqueur from the bottle. Her eyes riveted on his, across the room. Her heart bumped against her ribs, and she felt the sting of sudden tears. She felt like crying because she believed him.

"I haven't slept with another woman since I married you. In fact, since the first day I kissed you."

"You haven't?"

"I guess I'm a sucker when it comes to marriage vows."

The bottle of Bailey's thumped on the bar. She had almost dropped it from lifeless fingers as she watched him move toward her slowly. As she stood transfixed, he reached over the bar and took her hand. With gentle pressure, he guided her around the end of it until she stood directly in front of him. Then he laid his good hand on her shoulder and pressed down on it until her fanny touched the high stool behind her.

She was grateful for its support, because she

thought she might faint, both with relief at what he'd told her and with love. Oh, she could deny it, but when she drew her last breath she knew she would still be loving Jon Riley.

He parted her thighs and stepped between them, bringing their bodies close. She could feel his chest hairs against the clinging fabric of her tank top.

"In my misguided youth I thought sex was all for kicks. I was greedy, but aloof, you know?"

"Yes. I think so."

"It wasn't until I had made love with you that I knew what it was all about. And when you left me, mad as I was at you, I just couldn't bring myself to cheapen what we had shared. With anybody else it would have been a parody of the real thing."

He took a step closer. "Why would I want another woman, Brin, when I had you? Why would I even look for another woman, when I had loved the best? That isn't it, is it? Did you think I was being unfaithful to you?"

"No."

"Did someone tell you an outrageous lie about me and another woman?"

"No."

"Then what was it, sweetheart?" He lowered his head, bringing his face close to hers. His lips feathered over her neck, her earlobe. The bar caught her in the middle of her spine as she leaned back to give him access. "Why did you walk out on me?"

He kissed her mouth, but held back the passion that pulsed between them. He played at her lips with his, but restrained himself from claiming them in the way they both yearned for.

He raised her arms to the back of his neck and

crossed them. Then he traced the undersides of her arms downward, loving the involuntary moaning sound she made at his touch. His thumbs made a suggestive pass through her armpits. His hands paused, hovered, before the heels of them began to rub the sides of her breasts.

"What was it, Brin? Money?"

"Of course not."

He pressed into the fullness, forcing her breasts forward until the nipples made contact with his chest. Reflexively her thighs gripped his more tightly. The hair that sprinkled his legs tickled the smooth insides of her thighs.

"Work?"

"No."

"Then, what?"

Their lips finally met with the passion that had been promised. She caressed his tongue with hers as it delved into her mouth. His hands moved to the bottom of her tank top and began inching it up. Up, baring her navel. Up, baring her midriff. Up, baring the undercurves of her breasts. Up, until her breasts were flattened against the solid wall of his naked chest.

A low, mating sound rumbled in his throat as their kiss deepened. His hands splayed wide on her back. He drew her as close to him as possible, lifting her up until she stood on the lowest rung of the stool and was eye level with him. His lips were ravenous, his tongue rapacious, his hands unyielding. Their thighs pressed, rubbed, shifted against each other in a hungry desperation to gain ground.

Her womanhood tipped forward, instinctively seeking his hardness. His arousal was solid and hot as it pushed against his briefs. He plowed his hands into the waistband of her panties, covering her derriere with demanding fingers that urged her ever forward, ever closer. He gave in to the wildness streaking through him.

And then his tongue touched her nipple and her whole body went rigid with alarm.

No! She couldn't—*wouldn't*—let it happen. She'd have no ground left to stand on. The last seven months would mean nothing. If she made love to him, she would start eroding again.

She pushed him away and almost fell off the stool in her haste to escape his embrace. Turning her back, she leaned against the bar, bracing herself against it with straight arms while she gulped in air.

Riley stood behind her, his breathing just as labored as hers. He stared at her back, still bare because her top was hitched up. He tried to penetrate her brain, tried to understand the incomprehensible.

"*That's* it, isn't it?" Riley asked in a wheezing voice. Brin said nothing. "All right. So now I know." He took her by the shoulders and turned her around. Catching her cleft chin in his hand, he tilted her head back, forcing her to meet his eyes. "What went wrong with us in bed?"

# *Seven*

The telephone rang.

Had it been a bolt of lightning it couldn't have been more intrusive or electrifying. The moment was charged with emotion. Tension crackled like old paper.

Brin was the first to move. She pulled down her top with one swift tug and took a step toward the phone.

"Don't touch it," Riley barked.

"This is *my* house, *my* telephone. I'm answering it."

"You can't hide behind a telephone. We're going to have this discussion whether you answer that phone or not. And I swear to God that if Abel Winn is on the other end of that call, I'll tear the damn thing out of the wall!"

She glared up at him as she raised the receiver to

her ear. "Don't you dare bully me," she commanded him through clenched teeth. Then she said sweetly, "Hello?"

"Uh, Brin, were you asleep?"

"Whitney!"

Riley let loose a string of scathing profanities. Mentally Brin flinched. "Dim Whit?" he spat. "It's Dim Whit? I'll kill her." He curled his fingers and pantomimed choking somebody.

"Shh!"

"What?"

"Not you, Whitney."

"Is somebody with you? Golly, Brin, I'm sorry, I—"

"No, nobody's with me." Riley's ferocious scowl deepened and he reached for the phone. Brin dodged him in time. "Actually there is somebody with me, but . . . Oh, never mind, Whitney. It's a long story. Is something wrong?"

"Well, sort of."

"You'll have to speak louder. I can barely hear you. It's awfully noisy in the background." Brin turned her back on Riley, who was making vicious slicing motions across his throat with his index finger. Even if she hadn't worked in television she would have been able to interpret that hand cue.

"I'm at the airport," Whitney informed her.

"The airport! It's four o'clock in the morning."

"I know, and I'm sorry to be calling you now."

Brin dropped onto one of the barstools and propped her head in her hand in the posture of someone who doesn't know when the next brick is going to fall. What next? People didn't call from airports in the middle of the night for a friendly chat.

Calls originating from airports at four in the morning usually portended disaster.

"I went to New York to see my former roommate from Smith. I took the red-eye home. I got on the plane okay and . . ."

Riley nudged Brin's elbow. She looked up at him. Wearing an inquiring expression, he waggled the bottle of Bailey's in front of her. She shook her head. He shrugged, took up the brandy bottle, poured himself another generous draft and drank it down in one swallow. The potent liquor must have felt like a branding iron when it hit his stomach, because he made a comical expression of pain. He poured another two inches into the snifter and began to sip it slowly.

". . . and now I can't find it." Whitney Stone had just concluded her tale of woe, and Brin, having been distracted by Riley, had missed the essentials of it.

"Can't find what?"

"My purse. Say, Brin, are you sure you're okay? You sound funny. You weren't doing it or anything, were you?"

Brin's eyes slid up to Riley. He was watching her with the single-minded concentration of a cat on a trapped mouse. "No, nothing like that," Brin said uneasily. "You lost your purse?"

"Yes. It's gone. I can't find it anywhere."

Brin massaged her throbbing temples. She closed her eyes and wished for once that people didn't always count on her to be dependable, good ol' Brin.

"What's going on?" Riley demanded in a terse whisper.

Covering the mouthpiece Brin said, "She lost her purse."

"Brin?"

"Yes, Whitney, I'm still here. I'm trying to think. Did you check with the flight attendants?"

"They helped me search the plane after everybody got off."

"Somebody could have taken it."

"I don't think so. I don't remember getting on the plane with it."

"How could you get on an airplane without your purse?"

"Because she's d-u-m-b," Riley said, tapping his forehead with his index finger. "A space cadet."

Impatiently Brin waved her hand and mouthed "shut up" at him. "Weren't you carrying your boarding pass in it?"

"Don't fuss at me, Brin. I already feel like a fool."

Brin was immediately ashamed of herself. The younger woman was obviously close to tears and in need of help. Brin shouldn't have been so impatient with her. It certainly wasn't Whitney's fault that Riley was standing near-naked in front of her, looking like he was about to take a big bite of her. "All right, calm down. Crying won't help. What can I do?"

"Could you come get me?" Whitney asked in a small voice.

"At the airport? Now?" Brin asked in a high, reedy tone.

Now it was Riley's turn to wave his hands. He did it with considerably more gusto than Brin had. He waved them both, crisscrossing them in front of his body like a flagman aborting a landing attempt on an aircraft carrier. "No, no, no!" he hissed loud

enough for Brin to hear. "Nix. That idea is out."
She ignored him.

"I know it's asking a lot, Brin," Whitney was
saying.

"What about your parents?" Brin asked
hopefully.

"They went to Carmel for the weekend. Besides,
if they find out I've done something this stupid, I'll
catch hell."

"Do you need a place to stay? You can stay—"
She slapped away Riley's left hand as he reached
across her for the disconnect button on the phone.
". . . can stay . . ." They were engaged in an all out
hand-slapping contest now. "Hold on, Whitney."
Brin covered the mouthpiece again. "So help me,
Riley, if you don't leave this telephone alone and
mind your own business, I'll—"

"This *is* my own business."

"She called me, not you."

"If you invite her over here—"

"I repeat. *This is my house.* You can't tell me
what to do." She stared him down, then returned
to the girl on the phone. "Do you need a place to
stay?"

"No. The housekeeper is at home, but she won't
drive after dark, and even if she did, no one would
ride with her. I think she's certifiably blind. And if I
ask her to pay for a taxi, she's sure to tell my parents. Do you mind too much, Brin?"

Mind? Why should she mind? Already tonight
she had bickered with a recalcitrant caterer, dealt
with the sudden appearance of her estranged husband, who had had the unmitigated gall to crash
her party, diplomatically avoided the attentions of
a man she wanted to work for but whom she did

not want to become romantically involved with, rushed a bleeding man to the emergency room, played nurse to him while his hand was being sutured, and deflected his sexual advances while at the same time facing the dilemma of their crumbled marriage. What was one more catastrophe in light of all that? It was as if she were living through a bad episode of *The Twilight Zone.*

"Where are you?" She tried not to let her weariness and despondency show as she told Whitney to be watching for her car within the hour.

"You can't be serious," Riley said when she hung up and headed for the stairs.

"Don't badger me, Riley. She needs help."

With considerable emphasis, he set the snifter down on the bar. "I need help. You need help. Our marriage needs help."

"Our marriage has been on the back burner for seven months. One more hour won't hurt it."

He was right on her heels as she entered the bedroom. She went into the bathroom and pulled on the same jeans and sweat shirt she had worn earlier. Riley's blood had dried on them, but she was too tired to notice.

"I'll be back— What are you doing?"

"Trying my damnedest to put on my pants," he said from the edge of the bed, where he was seated, struggling to hold the jeans with one hand while he pushed his legs into them.

"You're not going anywhere."

"The hell I'm not. Do you think I'd let you drive out to the airport alone at four in the morning?"

"I don't need your protection."

"Don't pull a feminist act. Be reasonable. Anything could happen. You could have a flat tire."

She propped one fist on her hip. "You're the one who should be reasonable. If you can't even put on your pants, how much help do you think you'd be with a flat tire?"

"All right, Brin. Stand here and argue with me." He stood up, wriggling, trying to work the tight jeans over his hips without using his injured right hand. "But every second you waste here leaves Dim Whit out there alone with whatever perverts are lurking around the airport."

"You're actually concerned for her safety?"

"No, I'm concerned for the perverts'."

He had a point. And as she stood there ruminating on it, he managed to get into his shirt. "Button me up?"

He looked so damned adorable with his hair mussed and that boyish grin with the dimples at each end, Brin didn't know whether to kiss him or rake her nails down his face.

"Oh, all right," she said grudgingly. "Besides, I don't trust you here alone. No telling what you'd do while I was gone. You're worse than a three-year-old, who has to be watched every second." She virtually shoved the buttons through the holes, as though punishing them.

"Unless you want me to be exposing myself to Dim Whit, you'd better zip up my pants too."

She turned back and her gaze dropped to his fly. True. It was gaping open. In nervous reaction she wet her lips with her tongue.

He chuckled. "Gee, I'd like for you to, Brin. But I don't think we should take the time right now."

His joke made her mad. She drew her face into a taut, stern, no-nonsense mask and reached for the tab of the zipper. She yanked it upward.

"Ouch! Damn, Brin, be careful. You'll have to, uh . . ."

"No way."

"What's the matter?" he taunted. "Scared?"

"No!" she denied vehemently. "Aggravated. This wouldn't be a problem if you didn't wear your jeans so indecently tight."

"I never recall your complaining before. Come on, just a little pressure—"

"I know, I know." She nervously wet her lower lip again, daring him with her eyes to make another lewd comment. Then she thrust her hand between the folds of soft denim and pressed until she could easily slide the zipper up.

"There. See? No sweat." She felt his warm breath on the crown of her head, heard the amusement in his voice, and stepped away from him quickly. Turning on her heel, she proudly stalked from the room and down the stairs, not checking to see if he was following. He was. By the time she reached the back door, he was right behind her, stumbling down the back steps.

*Stumbling?*

She whirled around and peered up at him closely. His eyes were unnaturally bright. His smile was a shade crooked, and sappy. His lean cheeks were flushed. She reached up and put a hand on his forehead, but he didn't feel feverish.

"Whash a matter?" he asked.

Her eyes went round, then narrowed suspiciously. "You're plastered!"

He made an attempt at sobriety by pulling himself up straighter. "I am not. Jush a little, teeny-weeny bit woozshy from losh of blood." He held up his unsteady left hand, but had difficulty showing a fraction of an inch between his index finger and his thumb.

"Oh, for heaven's sake." None too gently Brin packed him into the front seat and fastened his seat belt.

By the time they were underway, his head was lolling on the back of the seat and his eyes were closed. "I must be crazy," Brin muttered to herself. "It's four o'clock in the morning. I'm driving through the streets of San Francisco with a drunk man while on my way to rescue a dimwit!"

To her surprise Riley chuckled, though his eyes remained closed. He reached across the interior of the car and patted her thigh. "You're a fine woman, Brin. A fine woman."

And because it felt so good riding there, she let his hand stay.

Brin saw Whitney before the younger woman spotted the car. She honked the horn, then stepped out onto the pavement and waved her arms, shouting Whitney's name. The girl came jogging toward her, lugging a suitcase.

"Brin, you'll never know how much I appreciate this. I don't know—Is that *blood*?"

"Uh, oh, yes."

"What happened?"

"It's a long story. Do you mind riding in the backseat?"

"No, sure." Whitney opened the rear car door and tossed her suitcase inside, scrambling in after it. "Were you hurt, Brin? Did you have an accident?"

"No, I—"

"Who's that? *Riley!*" Whitney shrieked.

Riley swore expansively, having been jarringly roused from his nap. He popped erect and bumped his head on the ceiling of the car. "Dammit!" His mumbled cursing continued as he turned to glower at the passenger in the back seat.

When he raised his hand to examine the bump on his head, Whitney cried, "Your hand! Did you hurt your hand? There's a bandage on it."

Riley shot Brin a look that said, "That's probably the most brilliant deduction she'll ever reach." To Whitney he said, "Yes, there's a bandage on it. And now I might have to get one on my head, thanks to you."

"I'm sorry, but I didn't see you sitting there. What happened to your hand?"

"It's a long story."

Whitney's round face puckered in perplexity. "That's what Brin said."

"I cut it on a broken glass and had to get stitches." Riley sighed and faced forward again, glad to have laid that matter to rest.

"Hmm," Whitney said. "Were you at Brin's house when it happened?"

"Yes," they chorused, looked at each other, then fell silent as they once again stared out the windshield.

"Were you two in bed when I called?" Whitney asked bluntly. Brin braked sharply. Riley laughed. Whitney clapped her hands together. "You *were?* You guys are back together? Oh, I'm so glad. I always said—"

"No, we're not back together," Brin interrupted. Maneuvering like a demolition driver, she swung the car onto the freeway.

"Oh." Whitney was obviously crestfallen. "Then why were you in bed together?"

"We weren't!" Brin cried. She now wished she

had let Riley talk her into staying at home and letting Whitney fend for herself.

"Well, it sounded like it," Whitney retorted defensively. "I heard all this scuffling and whispering and just, you know, *felt* like I had called at a bad time."

"It was a bad time because we *weren't* in bed together," Riley said.

After a short silence Whitney said, "Oh, I see."

"No, you don't." Brin looked in the rearview mirror to meet Whitney's eyes. "Riley and I are not getting back together," she said emphatically.

"Why not?"

"That's what I'd like to know," Riley chimed in, straightening from his slouch and looking at Brin's profile.

"It would be best for everybody if you two would reconcile your differences," Whitney said.

"Amen."

"Be quiet. You're drunk."

"He's *drinking* now?"

"I slept it off."

"You weren't asleep that long, and no, he's not *drinking*."

"I thought Riley had more character than to take to drinking."

"He hasn't taken to drinking!"

"Well, make up your mind, Brin."

"Yeah, make up your mind, Brin. You're the one who said I was drunk."

Brin emitted a short, loud whistle. "Look, guys, if we're going to take this show on the road, we're going to have to smooth out the dialogue." She had regressed from an episode of *The Twilight Zone* to an Abbott and Costello routine.

"If you two got back together it would certainly help the show," Whitney went on, obviously undaunted by Brin's shrinking supply of patience. "After what Daddy told me I can see why Riley would want to mend his fences."

Brin's head came around abruptly. "What about the show?"

Brin had stayed in contact with Whitney only because Whitney had assumed other responsibilities at the television station soon after Brin resigned her post as producer of *Riley in the Morning.* She couldn't have remained a confidante of Whitney's if the girl were still working in Riley's shadow. Not that Brin didn't trust her. She didn't think that Whitney Stone would maliciously carry tales about her back to Riley. But she knew how enamored Whitney was of him and how his charm could have swayed her into selling her own mother.

Brin's incisive question elicited diverse responses. Riley jerked as if he'd been shot, and snarled, "Nothing."

Whitney scooted forward so that she was sitting on the rim of the seat cushion, and folded her hands on the back of the front seat. "The show is in trouble."

"It's not in trouble," Riley countered.

"Well, Daddy says it is. Serious trouble. He said that ever since Brin left it's been sliding into the toilet. And that's a quote."

Brin hazarded a glance at Riley. He was looking at Whitney with murder in his eyes, but Whitney was so caught up in the subject that she didn't notice. It wasn't often that people looked to her as a source of valuable information. Now that she had an audience intent on hearing what she had to say, she was going to expound on her topic and enjoy every minute of the attention.

"What do you know about it?" Riley asked belligerently. "You're not even working on the show any longer. For that matter, what does 'Daddy' know? He's not back there. He doesn't know what I have to put up with to get every show on tape. Ineptitude. They've surrounded me with morons and expect me to overcome that."

"You could try harder to get along with people," Whitney said bravely. "You yell at everybody. Browbeat them until they're scared to death of you. I should know. And those producers—"

"Producers, plural?" Brin asked.

"He's run off three since you left."

"They were incompetent," Riley shouted. "One broad they hired, wore earrings that dangled down to her shoulders and a ring on every finger. I think she was into devil worship. I was interviewing gurus, fortune tellers, and witches every other day."

Brin bit back a laugh.

"Then they hired this jerk who had just graduated from Cal Tech with a degree in television. Hell, he'd never even seen the inside of a television studio. But to hear him tell it, he knew everything there was to know. He was telling engineers and technicians who had worked in TV for over twenty years how to do their jobs. And who did they bitch to? You got it. Me! The next one—"

"She ran out of the studio in tears," Whitney interrupted enthusiastically.

"What happened?"

Riley opened his mouth to speak, but Whitney

got there first. "I wasn't there, but if what everybody said was true, Riley was horribly cruel to her. And I didn't think she was *that* fat."

Brin looked at him with incredulity. "You called a woman fat? To her face? Riley, how could you?"

"I didn't call her fat," he snapped.

"Not exactly, no," Whitney conceded. "What he said was, 'Why don't you just park a battleship in front of the floor director when he's trying to give me time cues? I couldn't see around it any better than I can see around you.' "

"I sent her two dozen roses later, by way of apology," Riley grumbled. He slumped down in the seat, crossed his arms over his chest, hunched his shoulders forward, and looked like a little boy who was settling down for a long pouting spell.

"He hit a cameraman," Whitney reported.

"Hit?" Brin cried. She turned her head and stared at Riley. Finally he met her accusing stare.

"I didn't 'hit' him," he mumbled. "I just sort of . . . pushed him."

"Have you lost your mind? What's wrong with you?" Brin asked him. "Why would you hit *or* push anyone?"

Riley didn't see fit to answer, but Whitney did. "Because the guy told Riley that he would hand-deliver you to his bed if that would bring you back to the show and improve Riley's mood."

The silence in the car was thick. Whitney's eyes flew back and forth between the two of them. She adored them both, mainly because their lives seemed to contain the drama so lacking in hers.

Neither Brin nor Riley moved. They stared out the windshield, straight ahead. Whitney hadn't known what to expect when she imparted that last bit of information, but she was mildly disappointed that something drastic hadn't happened.

"This week Daddy told me that the station manager called Riley in on the carpet and told him he'd better get his act together. No pun intended. He told Riley to find a producer he can work with and bring the ratings of the show up to where they should be . . . or else."

She didn't need to explain what the "or else" was. "Or else" could only mean cancellation. Professional death.

"Why isn't anybody saying anything?" Whitney asked after a ponderous silence. "You're not mad at me are you, Riley?"

He drew in a long breath and released it on a sigh. "No, Whitney. I'm not mad at you."

"Brin is still your wife. She should know what's going on in your life. You two are my favorite people in the whole world. I want you to be happy. Living apart like this is silly."

"I . . . we appreciate your concern," Riley said quickly. He gave Whitney a soft smile, which ordinarily would have made Brin love him even more. "Be sure to notify the credit-card companies tomorrow that your purse was lost."

"I will, Riley, I will," Whitney said worshipfully.

"You must learn to be more careful. There are some bad characters roaming around who prey on absentminded young women. I'd hate like hell for anything to happen to you."

"You . . . you would?" she sputtered.

"Of course. What would I do without my Dim Whit?"

The smile Whitney gave back to him was radiant. Brin brought the car to the curb outside the

Stones' impressive house. She hadn't had to ask directions. She and Riley had come here to a company Christmas party. "Do you need any help with your bag?" Brin asked Whitney. She tried to appear calm and unaffected by all that Whitney had said, but it was difficult.

"No, thanks," Whitney replied, opening the door and climbing out, dragging the suitcase with her. She bent down and spoke through the window in a soft voice. "Brin, you're not angry with me for speaking my mind, are you? You know how I feel about you. I think you're super. You're the only person who ever treated me like I wasn't a doormat. And even though Riley has yelled at me on occasion, I know he really likes me."

"Yes, he does. I know he does." Brin patted Whitney's hand reassuringly.

"I didn't mean to butt in. I just want you two back together because I know you love each other."

"It's not that simple, but as Riley said, we appreciate your concern."

"Well, thanks again for the ride."

"Good night."

"Good night."

Brin kept the car idling at the curb until they saw that she was safely inside and in the housekeeper's care. Then Brin turned the car homeward. Riley had either fallen asleep or was pretending to be. In any event, they didn't speak on the trip back. Brin was fighting a battle not to cry. She was angry. Furious, in fact. And hurt. The pain of humiliation ate at her vitals like a carrion bird.

When they were several blocks from their destination, she said, "I'm going to drop you off at your place."

"*Our* place," Riley corrected her sourly. "And you can't do that, because my car's still at your friend's house. Besides, I told you this predawn expedition isn't going to keep us from having our discussion."

She tried not to let him know how furious she was, but as soon as the kitchen door was closed behind them, she unleashed her wrath.

"You bastard!" she began without preamble. "When I think about . . ." Too angry to continue, she marched the length of the kitchen, then back. Her shoes crunched on the broken glass. "Now I know why you didn't want me to see Whitney tonight."

If there was a remnant of brandy-induced inebriation left in Riley, it was burned away by her anger. He assumed an arrogant stance, one knee bent, hands on hips, head cocked to one side. "Just what the hell are you talking about? What has Whitney got to do with anything? I want to know why when I kissed you—"

"You were afraid she would spill the beans."

"Beans?"

"And you should have seen your face when she did."

"What?" He was getting angry in his own right.

"Since you showed up here unannounced and unwelcome, you've been whining about how you've missed me. How you love me. How you want me back." She rounded on him, her cleft chin jutting forward. "Tell me, Mr. Riley. Do you want me back as your wife or as your *producer*?"

If she had socked him in the gut he couldn't have seemed more surprised. His breath whooshed out, and an expression of absolute disbelief came over his face. "Is *that* what you think this is all about?"

"Yes!"

"Well, you couldn't be more wrong."

"Am I? *Am I?*" She began pacing again, thumping her clenched fists on her thighs as though barely preventing them from striking out at something; namely, his handsome face. "When I think what a fool I've been, when I think about how close I came to being lured into your web again, I could scream."

She bristled with anger as she faced him. "You don't want me back because you love *me*. You want me back because you love *yourself*. You want me back to save your skin. Your all-important career is on the line and you want me to save it for you.

"You don't want me back in your bed nearly as much as you want me back in your studio handling petrified or petulant guests, keeping the crew in line, taking care of the million and one details of producing a daily television talk show. The mighty star can't be bothered with such piddling details, so he becomes a penitent for one night. That's what all this has been for, hasn't it, Riley? It wasn't just coincidence that brought you to me on the night I was making an important career decision."

He denied her allegations so softly, it was unsettling. "You're wrong, Brin."

"I don't think so."

"You are."

"You expect me to believe that if *Riley in the Morning* were doing well in the ratings, if everything were just superkeen at the television station, if your job weren't in jeopardy, you'd still have come here tonight begging me for a reconciliation?"

"It's true."

"Oh, I'll bet. Tell you what, Riley, you can choose." She tossed her head back haughtily. "Do you want me to come back as your producer? Or do you want me as your wife?"

"Both." He closed the distance between them and took her shoulders between his hands, even though he winced with the pain it caused his right hand. "What's wrong with having both? We were a good team in the studio. A better one at home. A terrific one in bed." The focus of his eyes sharpened, and they seemed to drill into her. "Which brings us back to our original argument. What happened to all that fantastic sex?"

"I don't want to talk about it," she said tightly, growing stiff beneath his hands.

"Well, that's just too damn bad, because I do and we are. That's the crux of the problem. That's what went wrong with our marriage, and I don't intend to deny or ignore it. I want to know why. Why? Why wasn't it good for us any more? I remember the first night I noticed that something was wrong. It was the night of the Press Club's award program."

As painful as it would be, Brin knew he was going to make them run this gauntlet. He wasn't going to leave her alone until they talked about that night and the ones that had followed. . . .

# *Eight*

"Oh, Riley!" Brin gripped his knee beneath the table when the master of ceremonies announced that the Press Club had voted *Riley in the Morning* the best of local television programming.

Grinning from ear to ear, Riley leaned over and kissed her, then stood and made his way through the banquet tables that filled the largest ballroom of the Fairmont Hotel. On the dais he accepted the coveted award, to a standing ovation.

"Mr. Mayor, fellow members of the media"—he drew in a deep breath and released it on an unsteady laugh—"this is terrific!" His speech was endearing and self-effacing. He publicly thanked the management of the television station, his crew and technicians, most of all his producer.

"I guess all those ideas we talked over in bed paid

off, honey." Everyone laughed and glanced in Brin's direction.

And that was the last time that evening that anyone looked at her, or even acknowledged that she existed, much less that she was the mastermind behind the show's innovative programming.

Riley was photographed until he held up his hand in front of his eyes and said, "You've all turned purple." Everyone within hearing distance thought that was hilariously funny and commented that his spontaneous wit was no doubt one reason for his success.

Though everyone else seemed to have forgotten that Brin and Riley were a team, he hadn't. He called her forth out of the crowd to meet the mayor. "Mr. Mayor, I'd like to introduce my producer and wife, Brin."

She extended her hand, but instead of shaking it, the mayor clasped it warmly between his and patted it. "This is a pleasure, Mrs. Riley. Riley, you've got a mighty pretty little lady here."

"Thank you. I think so." Riley's arm went around her shoulders with proud possession. Apparently he didn't notice her rigid posture or strained smile. Probably because at that moment he was called away for another round of picture-taking.

"Wow, what a night," he said once they were in their car and on the way home. He loosened his tie and unfastened the collar button of his shirt. "She's a beauty, isn't she?" With his free hand he held up the gold statue of a woman. His name and the date were engraved on the shield she held in her hands at waist level.

"Yes, she is," Brin admitted. She hated herself for harboring these resentful feelings. But she was hurt and felt overlooked, inconsequential, and insignificant. Had she truly been slighted, or was her ego making her feel as though she had been? Was this as important as it seemed to be, or was her imagination blowing it way out of proportion?

Riley didn't notice that she was unusually quiet. He chatted on about the evening, about who had been in attendance, others who had won awards in various fields of journalism, the banquet food, the emcee's stale jokes.

Not until they were in bed did he get an indication that something wasn't right. He was tipsy on champagne and happiness and reached for her beneath the covers, ready for a private celebration of his success.

She went into his arms willingly enough. She even kissed him back with all the fervor in her heart. But he didn't notice that when he drew her closer against him, and she rested her head on his shoulder, she squeezed tears from her eyes.

His hand moved caressingly over her breasts. "I'm sorry, darling," she said quickly, lifting his hand away, "I don't think I'm up to it tonight."

He raised his head immediately and looked down at her with concern. "Brin? What's the matter? Are you sick? Why didn't you tell me? Do you need anything?"

"No, no, I'm not sick." She touched his chest, but immediately removed her hand. "I just don't feel very well." She couldn't bring herself to say she had a headache. She wasn't about to resort to that cliché.

He smiled in understanding and pressed his hand against her lower abdomen. "Having your period?"

She shook her head, biting back the groan of pleasure that issued up through her throat at the touch of his hand. "No. I just . . . would you mind if we didn't tonight?"

"Of course not. I'm not a surly beast." He kissed her mouth softly and turned her so that her bottom was tucked against his lap and his thighs were supporting the backs of hers. His arms wrapped around her, and his breath stirred her hair as he whispered, "Just let me hold you. You're so cuddly and warm. I love just holding you." He kissed the back of her neck. "I love you."

"I love you too."

And she did. That was why her shame at what she was feeling tasted so brassy and bitter on her tongue. . . .

"Professional jealousy?"

Genuine disbelief was stamped on Riley's features as he gazed up at her from the foot of the bed, where he was sitting. As they had reconsidered that evening, which had represented a major turning point in their happy marriage, they had moved from the kitchen, through the living room, and upstairs to the bedroom, as though migrating toward the source of their problem.

"You left because you were jealous of my success?"

"I knew that was what you would think." Brin turned her back on him and went to the dressing table, sitting down and gazing at her reflection in the mirror. She was mildly surprised to see that she was still wearing the diamond studs in her ears that she had worn for the party. They were a laughable contrast to her blood-stained sweat shirt.

Her face was lined with fatigue. She was extremely tired, and knew that most of it was mental weariness. She had been thinking too much and too long tonight. Picking up a hairbrush, she dragged it through her hair. "That's why I didn't want to talk to you about this, Riley. I knew you'd dismiss it as jealousy and consider me a fool."

"I could never consider you a fool, Brin. And I'd hardly 'dismiss' the decline of my marriage."

"For seven months you did." Her tone was sharper than she had intended.

He seemed almost ready to refute her accusation, but he closed his lips and let his head fall forward. "You've got me there, Brin. I should have come after you sooner. I wanted to. There hasn't been a day when I didn't have to talk myself out of coming after you and dragging you home—by the hair on your head if necessary." He raised his head and met her eyes in the mirror. "I was too damn mad at first, then too damn proud."

"A big television star doesn't go groveling to his estranged wife, begging her to come back to him."

"Something like that, yeah." He got up and began pacing the width of the room. She saw him unconsciously nursing his right hand.

"Does your hand hurt?"

"Yes, but that doesn't matter."

"Why don't you take one of those pain pills the doctor sent home with me?"

"Because I don't want my brain to be dulled. I want to get to the bottom of this. I need to understand it." He rubbed his eye sockets with the thumb and index finger of his left hand. "Let me get this straight. You were turned off sex that night because I won the award. Right?"

"Wrong." She laid the hairbrush aside and swiveled around on the dressing-table stool to face him. "Don't you know how proud I was of you?"

"I thought so at the time."

"I was. I still am. I guess I resented the fact that I didn't share the award. I felt at least partially responsible for the success of *Riley in the Morning*. Call it proud, call it selfish, call it presumptuous, but that's how I felt."

"So did I, Brin! You were responsible. I recognized you from the podium during my acceptance speech. You *were* the brains behind the show's comeback. Didn't I make that clear? Did I make you feel otherwise?"

"No, but everyone else did. You were the one photographed and interviewed. You—"

"You mean that if some photographer had asked to take your picture that night, my marriage wouldn't have broken up and we wouldn't be having this discussion right now?"

She counted to ten slowly. "Please don't insult me, Riley. Of course it's not that easily explained. That night was only the culmination of many. Every time someone looked past me to see you, I felt a bit of myself chipping away. I felt myself diminishing."

"Public recognition goes with my job, Brin," he said softly.

"I know that, and I wasn't disturbed because fans weren't clamoring for my autograph. There was room for only one star in the family and you were it. I didn't want to be the star. I didn't want to share the limelight. It's just that I didn't want to be invisible, either."

She got off the stool and needlessly began straightening the covers on the bed. She needed activity, movement, or she was going to explode. Besides, when she looked at him, she found it near to impossible to voice her thoughts.

"After months of diligent, hard work, after the ratings had been pulled up, and after *Riley in the Morning* had become a show the competitors had to contend with, I was reduced to being Mrs. Riley. Not Brin Cassidy, producer. But only an append-age of yours. A virtually useless, invisible one, I might add."

"You are my wife, Brin. You shouldn't have agreed to marry me if you didn't want to be Mrs. Riley."

"I *did* want to be. But I am a *woman*, not merely a wife. I wanted to be your wife and your producer, recognized as both, not only as the pretty little lady standing just outside your spotlight."

"I never thought of you that way. Sometimes I act chauvinistic just to get a rise out of you, but you know I'm not really that backward. You know bet-ter than to accuse me of that."

"You didn't think that way, but everyone else did."

"And that's why you started freezing up in bed? Not because of what I thought, but because of what other people thought?"

"How was I to compete?" she asked, rounding on him, frustrated at his obtuseness, his inability to see her point.

"Compete? I don't understand."

"You should see yourself in public, Riley. You

revel in celebrity. You love the attention and the acclaim. And the louder the applause, the better you like it."

"You knew that about me before you married me. At this late date am I supposed to apologize for that aspect of my personality?"

"No. I love that part of you too."

"Then what are we fighting about? Heaven above, I must be getting as dense as Dim Whit!"

Brin drew a deep breath, hoping that she could make her feelings clear to him. "That night when we got home, you were higher than a kite. Drunk on celebrity. You had basked in all that adulation. Your enjoyment of it was almost orgasmic."

"I was happy. Wasn't I supposed to be?" Impatience made his voice louder.

"Yes, of course."

"Then why should you feel threatened?" he nearly shouted.

"What could I do to you in bed that would make you feel that good?"

Stupefied, he stared at her. Gradually he lowered himself to the bed. "God." He covered his face with his left hand and dragged it down over his features until one by one his fingers trailed off his chin.

When he looked up at her again, his eyes were bleak. "You thought sex with you wouldn't be as good as winning some damn statue?"

"What could I do to top it?"

His shoulders slumped defeatedly, and he shook his head in bafflement. "That's comparing apples and oranges, Brin."

"It didn't seem so at the time. I felt thoroughly inadequate."

"You make me sound like an egomaniac, who made impossible demands on you."

"I don't mean to," she said, her tone and expression softening. She came to stand close to the foot of the bed, where he sat. "Oh, you have a healthy ego, all right, but this was my problem, my psychological trauma, not yours."

"It's *our* problem, Brin. Why didn't you tell me any of this? Why didn't you discuss what you were feeling?"

"Because I knew it would sound like sour grapes. I knew you would think I was just jealous of your high public profile."

"And you aren't?" he asked teasingly.

She laughed softly. "Not in the way you mean. I resented it sometimes."

"What times?"

She could tell that he had a sincere wish to know. "Your audience sees you only when you're perfect. Perfectly groomed, perfectly happy, perfectly everything. But I saw you when you looked like hell, when you got out of bed, before your first cup of coffee, when you slouched around the house in grubby clothes. I held your head over the commode that time you got a stomach virus. I washed your dirty socks."

"But I folded them," he said, holding up an index finger. Her smile never quite reached her eyes. "I see your point, though," he said softly. "I'll admit I never thought of it that way."

"I guess I resented everyone thinking you were perfect when I knew better. Sometimes, in my most paranoid moments, I thought that you saved your perfection for everyone else and I got the leftovers."

"I was never as good as when I was with you, Brin." He reached for her hand and squeezed it. With a gentle pressure, he urged her down on the bed beside him. They sat there, shoulders touching. "Think back to that first day you reported to work. As you so impolitely pointed out, I was a mess. I had bags under my eyes; I was doing shoddy interviews. I had grown placid, which is death for anybody on television. You whipped me into shape. And if no one, me included, gave you credit for that, we were at fault."

"Is that all I wanted? Credit? Yes, I suppose so," she said, answering her own question. "Now that sounds so crass and selfish, so shallow."

"You wanted sensitivity from your husband, which is what any woman has a right to expect. John Q. Public is basically a stupid animal. Don't blame him for being insensitive. Place the blame where it belongs. With me.

"I should have realized what you were feeling and done something about it. I *am* a conceited, self-centered bastard. There I was, soaking up the glory, while you were hurting. In this case, ignorance was not bliss. I should have come to you on bended knees, in gratitude, thanking you for what you'd done for me. Instead I crawled into bed that night expecting you to give even more of yourself to me, to make yourself accessible for my pleasure and well-being." He touched her hair. "No wonder you were turned off sex."

"I was never turned off sex."

"You could have fooled me."

"Don't you see, Riley? I was afraid I wouldn't measure up. You had thousands of women idolizing you. But you were no idol to me. I knew you were fallible." She spread her hands wide, palms up, as though giving him a humble offering. "I merely loved you. In spite of your imperfections. I loved you so much it hurt. So much that I didn't want to fail you. And if I couldn't match that high you got from your adoring fans, that would be my failure."

"So you stopped trying."

"I guess that's right."

He stood up and ambled around the room as though looking for a place to light. It was a familiar tactic he used when trying to arrange his thoughts. Brin sat where he had left her, waiting for him to speak.

"I couldn't figure it out. At first I thought I was just catching you on off days. Before, we had always laughed about it when one or the other of us was sexually out of sync. You weren't laughing any longer."

He paused in front of her dressing table. He picked up the hairbrush she had used minutes earlier, and lightly slapped it against his palm. "Finally—sometimes I'm not too astute and have to be hit over the head with a two-by-four before I catch on—I realized that you weren't interested in sex at all. Zilch. Zero."

"I wasn't sure you even noticed."

He laughed mirthlessly. "Oh, I noticed, but I pretended not to. I was shaking in my boots. Scared . . . well, scared. I didn't want to face what was so painfully clear."

"Which was?"

"That I couldn't make my wife happy in bed." He was facing the mirror. Now he raised his eyes to meet her reflection. "You seem surprised," he said when he saw her expression.

"I'm stunned. How could you think that?"

He turned around. "Brin, when a man touches a woman and she cringes, it's a pretty good indication that she doesn't either like or want his touch."

"Did I do that?" she asked in a small voice.

"At first your turn-off wasn't so obvious. You just became this brisk, businesslike creature who never slowed down long enough for me to get my arms around, who never had time for a kiss, whose conversation centered around *Riley in the Morning* or there wasn't any conversation at all, who was so exhausted from the way she was driving herself that when we did get into bed she fell asleep instantly. Or pretended to."

"You make me sound like a machine."

"That's what you were, a machine who looked and sounded like Brin, beautiful, sexy, intelligent Brin. But I didn't know you anymore. And I was lost. I didn't have an instruction booklet on how to operate this new machine. Nothing I did seemed to work."

He laughed ruefully as he toyed with the perfume decanters on her dresser. "The happy-go-lucky approach fell flat, because your sense of humor seemed to have evaporated. The romantic approach was hard to pull off, because I couldn't even get near you without the invisible barriers going up. And once, when I tried the caveman approach by reaching around you and covering your breasts with my hands, you fought me off and made me feel like I had a contagious disease."

Brin's eyes were brimming with tears. She looked down to find that her fingers were threaded together tensely in her lap. "I wanted you to touch me, Riley. I wanted to make love with you. But I just couldn't risk it."

"Do you have any idea what it does to a man when he thinks he can't please his wife?"

"I imagine it's terrible."

"Hell on earth."

"It couldn't have been good for your star's ego."

"It would have been just as devastating if I'd been a ditch digger. I tormented myself for hours analyzing what was wrong. Was I too passionate? Not passionate enough? Did I want sex too frequently? Not frequently enough? Was our bedroom scene too kinky? Not kinky enough? Did my body revolt you? Was I too small to satisfy you?"

"Oh, Riley," she said, shaking her head and laughing scoffingly.

"Well, that's what goes through a man's head!" he cried defensively. "All I had to go on were the signals you were transmitting. And what I interpreted them to mean was that you wanted nothing to do with me in bed."

"Why didn't you ask me what was wrong?"

"Do you think I wanted to hear you say that I was too small?"

For the first time in months, they laughed together. It sounded good. It felt good. But when the laughter subsided Riley said seriously, "For two people who have made careers in the communications field, we certainly didn't communicate, did we?"

"No. We didn't."

"I was afraid to broach the subject for fear of what I'd hear."

"And I couldn't broach it because I thought you'd

ridicule me for being jealous and petty. And I swear to you, Riley," Brin said with complete sincerity, "that wasn't the reason."

"Clarify it for me one more time. I want to be sure I understand why you left."

"I was afraid that if I stayed with you I'd continue to lose ground, that I would eventually become no more to you than a shadow, that I would lose all sense of my own identity. Before long I'd become boring to you and therefore dispensable. When I went to work for *Riley in the Morning*, the show needed me. You needed me. Once I put you on top, I was afraid you wouldn't need me anymore, professionally or otherwise."

"You were wrong. Very wrong."

"Whether I was or not, that's how I perceived the situation, and we generally act on our perceptions, not on actualities."

Slowly he walked toward the bed, and crouched in front of her. "So where does that leave us?"

She sighed. "I don't know."

"Are you going to accept Winn's job this morning?"

"I don't know that either," she said with a note of desperation. "But if I do, I want you to understand one thing, Riley. There has never been, or ever will be, anything personal between Abel and me."

He looked chagrined. "In light of our recent conversation I think you can see why I suspected that there might be some passion simmering there."

"Never. At least not on my part."

"He's reputedly a hotshot in boardrooms and bedrooms."

"So are you."

His eyes lit up. "Yeah?"

"Fishing for compliments? Don't expect me to stroke your inflated ego, Mr. Riley."

"Could you?"

"Oh, yes," she answered after a cautious pause. "I certainly could."

"How, Brin?"

She must be awfully tired. Because she rarely wept except when she was very tired, and she was dangerously close to tears now. Reaching out, she brushed the silver-tipped hair off his forehead. "I could tell you that no man compares to you, that I've never been attracted to another man the way I was to you from the very beginning, that your kisses are to die for." She smiled a gamine smile and leaned forward to whisper, "Your body is nothing less than magnificent and you certainly aren't too small!"

"Whew! That's a relief."

Laughing softly, they bumped foreheads, then noses. They stayed like that, exchanging breaths. At last he tilted his head to one side and grazed her lips with his. It was a kiss as gentle as a spring rain.

"Do you know what it felt like when you left me?"

"I wasn't proud of the way I went about it. I took the coward's way out."

"You had stayed home from work that day, saying you were sick. I called several times during the day to check on you."

"I didn't answer the phone."

"Which worried the hell out of me. Then when I came home and found all your things gone and your note . . . well, it was like I'd been hit by a Mack truck."

She pinched her eyes closed and shuddered as she inhaled jaggedly. "I'm so sorry."

"That night I was in a stupor. I kept asking myself what I'd done wrong and made grandiose plans about how to win you back. But the next day when I got your letter saying you weren't coming back no matter what, I flew into a rage."

"What did you do?"

He joined her on the edge of the bed. "I went out on the patio and, bent on destroying something, uprooted all those plants you'd had me set out."

"Those things cost five ninety-nine apiece!" she cried.

"At that point I didn't care. Made a helluva mess. Then I got blind, stinking drunk."

"So did I."

"You did?"

"Not blind, stinking, but morosely so."

"I got angry enough to wait you out, to defy your desertion. You walked out? Fine, good, see if I care." He shook his head sadly. "But life just wasn't fun any more. You'd taken all the color with you. Everything was gray. From time to time I'd forget what had happened and would turn to you to share a comment about a book or a movie or a TV show or a flavor of ice cream. Only you weren't there, Brin, and I would lose all pleasure in it."

He combed his fingers through her hair. "I wanted you back at any cost, but my damnable pride kept me from coming after you. And each day that passed made it harder to come begging."

"I missed you too," she confessed quietly. "It was scary. Suddenly nothing in my life was familiar, not my job, or where I lived. But I couldn't come back, either. In the first place I wasn't sure you wanted me back. And if you did, what would have been the point of leaving? What would I have proved?"

"And now? Have you proved what you wanted to, that I can't or don't want to live without you?"

"That wasn't my intention. I set out to prove that I could be a whole, viable person without Jon Riley."

"You always were, Brin. God forgive me for making you feel that you weren't." He cupped her face between his hands and stroked her lips with his thumbs. "Abel Winn is offering you the moon. I hate the bastard for being capable of doing that, but that's life. You'd be crazy not to take that job."

"It's not morning yet. I haven't made up my mind."

"That's the advantage I'm pressing. He's not here with you tonight. I am. You're still my wife. I want you back in my life. I love you. So stay with me tonight. Share my bed. Lie with me. No sex. Just be near. I think we owe that much to each other."

"And what will happen in the morning if I do accept Winn's job?"

"I'll let you go and wish you well. I swear it."

Why did she hesitate to give him an answer? She believed him. He would live with her decision. Why, then, was she terrified to share a bed with him for the remainder of the night?

Because she still loved him. And because love sometimes paid no attention to wisdom.

Granted, she was seeing their marriage from a different angle. Riley was still her husband. She *did* owe him this night. And she owed it to herself, because she had to be sure. If she did decide to take the job in Los Angeles, which would be tantamount to divorcing Riley, she had to be certain that she was emotionally, as well as physically, free of him.

"All right, Riley," she said softly. "Let's go to bed."

They undressed slowly, watching each other. As bodies were unclad and skin was uncovered, they had a difficult time keeping libidos under control.

"I think you'd better stop there," Riley said thickly. She was down to the tank top and panties.

She nodded in agreement and was glad he had left on his briefs. He switched off the lamp. Habit placed her on his right side. As soon as the covers were pulled over them, they rolled to face each other, as they always had.

"Be careful of your hand."

He rested it above her head on the pillow. "It's practically well by now."

Brin knew he was lying. His lips were still rimmed with that telltale fine white line. "Sure you won't take a pill?"

"And miss any of this? Not likely." He wove their legs together and inched closer.

She laid her hand on his neck. "You should get some sleep."

"I don't want to." His protest was belied by his eyelids, which were struggling to stay open. The events of the night had exacted their toll. He was putting up a valiant battle to stave off their effects.

"But you need to rest," Brin whispered. She curled her hand around his head and pulled it down to her breasts.

He nestled there, butting his head against the soft flesh until he found a familiar spot. "You don't play fair," he mumbled sleepily.

"Shh." Her fingers sifted through his hair. "Go to sleep."

Within minutes she could tell by his even breathing that he had lost his fight and was asleep. But Brin lay awake. She had only a few hours to make up her mind and she still didn't know what her answer to either man would be.

The job with Winn was tantalizing. The money was more than adequate. It would be exciting to get in on the ground floor of a new, nationally syndicated show. She had never been able to resist a challenge like that.

But she didn't really want to move to Los Angeles. Money wasn't everything. *Riley in the Morning* had never failed to stimulate her creative juices and keep her excitement level at its peak. What could be more challenging than making a successful marriage?

And she loved Riley.

She rested her chin on his head and hugged it tight against her. She loved Riley. At that moment she couldn't think of anything more tantalizing than sleeping with him every night. He was more fun to be with than anybody she'd ever known. He acted a bit petulant at times, but that ornery streak in him appealed to her maternal instincts. And she could be a real bitch when she put her mind to it. He'd always handled her darker moods with uncanny tolerance, patiently coaxing her out of them with laughter.

She wanted *Riley in the Morning* and she wanted Riley.

So what was keeping her from committing herself to that decision? Only one thing: Why had he chosen tonight to seek reconciliation?

Was it because he couldn't stand another day without her, or because he'd been handed down an ultimatum? Did he want his wife back? Or his producer? Was his marriage more important? Or the future of his television show? Whom did he love the most, himself or her?

Did it matter?

Her fingers closed around a handful of his precious hair. Whom had *she* loved the most when she'd walked out on him? Whom had she been preoccupied with? Whose well-being had been foremost in her mind?

Yet he had swallowed his monumental pride and come after her. He had recognized and admitted that they were far better off with than without each other. Certainly there were problems inherent in any two-career marriage. If Riley had the courage to meet them head-on, didn't she?

Brin kissed the top of his head, his shoulder. But he didn't wake up. Not even when she left the bed and crept downstairs.

# Nine

"Brin?"

"Hmm?"

"Did you get up?"

"Yes. I went downstairs for a while."

"What for?"

"I got the coffee ready and set the timer."

"What time is it?"

"Early. I'm sorry I woke you up."

"It's okay. I'm glad you did."

As she resumed her spot beside him, their legs automatically interlaced. She snuggled close to his chest, burying one hand in his armpit. His left arm went around her waist.

"Does your hand hurt?"

"Maybe," he answered dreamily. "I can't feel anything but you." For several moments nothing disturbed the dawn-quiet silence in the house except their gentle breathing. Then he said, "You feel so good against me. You always did."

"I'm glad you think so."

"One of the first things I noticed was how physically compatible we are."

"I noticed that too," she said, smiling against his chest. The soft, crinkly hairs tickled her lips.

"God, I've missed holding you. Just holding you. It feels so good." He tried to draw her closer, though that was impossible. He rubbed his cheek against the crown of her head. When he relaxed his hold a fraction, she tilted her head back in order to look up at him.

"It feels good to be held."

A spasm of emotion flickered over his face. His deep blue eyes burned into hers. They took in her delicate complexion, which the first morning light only made more pearlescent. Her hair formed a wreath of tangled, inky curls around her face. The long lashes surrounding her aquamarine eyes were dark and luxuriant. Her lips were rosy and moist and looked ready to engage in any activity suggested. As always, the cleft in her chin bewitched him. She looked wanton. Willing. Tousled sexiness incarnate.

He whispered her name huskily before his mouth moved down to hers. Lips touched. Parted. Touched again. And again. Then clung. His tongue shyly pried her lips open. Investigated.

Brin, yearning and pliant, arched her body against his and curved her hand around the back of his head. He needed no further encouragement. His tongue spiraled down deep into the hollow of her mouth. It wasn't hurried or abusive or plundering. It wasn't apologetic or timid either. But questing, seeking, reacquainting itself with every sweet nuance of her mouth.

He whispered incoherently as his lips skittered over her face, brushing airy kisses on her forehead and eyelids and cheeks and nose. But always his lips came back to hers. He nibbled at them, catching her provocative lower lip lightly between his teeth, worried it gently, then soothed it with damp sweeps of his tongue. He tasted the smile that tugged at the corners of her lips. His kisses were wild and controlled, rowdy and tender, capricious and lazy, playful and passionate. Ever changing, ever evocative.

"You have the mouth I fantasized about in my youth," he growled softly.

"What makes it special?"

"Everything. The taste, the shape, the way it responds. I love it."

He kissed her again until they were both breathless.

"You're an excellent kisser," Brin murmured drowsily, as though his mouth had siphoned all the energy out of her. "Every woman should know what it's like to be kissed by you at least once."

"What's it like?" His lips rubbed against hers.

"Like being made love to."

"The very act?"

"The very act. Your kisses say that you're definitely the man, I'm the woman. No matter the tempo, they're never sloppy. Always thorough. Your kisses leave me weak, yet terribly aroused."

He raised his head high enough to gaze down at her. A groove formed between his brows as his index finger circled her mouth where the skin had turned rosy. "My beard—"

"It doesn't matter." As though it weighed a thousand pounds, she lifted her hand and stroked his chin, where a morning stubble bristled, shadowing the lower half of his face. "It's rather piratical. And I've always had a hankering to be taken by a pirate."

"Why's that?" The backs of his fingers strummed the column of her throat.

"I'm not sure. I think it has something to do with his sword."

He suspended his love play to angle his head back and look down at her cynically. "His sword, huh?"

"Um-hm." She smiled suggestively.

He touched his lips to her ear and whispered something naughty. She giggled, then swatted his bare shoulder playfully. They engaged in a skirmish of slapping hands and harmless nibbling teeth. When it ended, their mouths were hotly fused again and both considered themselves the victor.

Playfulness gave way to passion. With a low groan, Riley stretched out his legs. Taking the subtle cue, Brin straightened her knees. They moved together until they were toe to toe, shin to shin, thigh to thigh. When their loins met, the heat spread up through them like spilling lava.

She gasped his name.

He sighed hers.

He crooked one arm around her neck and bent her head back over it while his mouth savored hers. His other hand splayed wide over the small of her back, anchoring the yielding feminine delta against his swollen sex.

Moans of mutual satisfaction welcomed the first

pinkish rays of light that filtered through the shutters into the room.

"I missed you, Brin." His breath was hot against her neck. He poured love words into her ear like a healing elixir. "I missed this. I missed having you in my bed, missed your passion. Sometimes I thought I would die if I could never hold you like this again. I needed you so much I wanted to die. Missing you was a physical illness. Make me well," he ended on an urgent plea. "Make me well."

His hand slipped inside her panties. Strong, warm fingers kneaded the firm flesh of her derriere, urging her closer. She wedged her hand between their bodies and curled her fingers into the elastic waistband of his underwear. She felt him stop breathing. Time stood still for a moment while their hearts thumped together.

Then her hand moved. Peeling the briefs down, she freed him. He let his breath go with a sound that was part sigh, part moan. He was hard and smooth and velvety against her thighs.

Impatiently his hand grappled with her panties and worked them down past her hips. She kept her legs pressed together tightly because she knew he loved a challenge and because his probing against the downy cleft at the top of her thighs was immensely pleasurable.

Instinctively she turned onto her back. An urge as old as mankind directed him to follow, to cover. His hands scoured her restlessly, almost desperate in their need to touch her flesh. Mindless of the bandage that wrapped his right hand, mindless of the painful wound beneath it, he caressed her.

With a wild recklessness, he took the hem of the tank top in both hands and pulled it over her head.

He flung it aside viciously. With legs pumping as rapidly as pistons, he shoved his underwear down his legs and kicked it away. Levering himself above her with straight, rigid arms, his eyes devoured her naked body.

Then, only then, did he regain his senses. He blinked to clear his eyes of a passion-induced blindness.

"Don't stop there, Riley," she gasped.

He laughed softly. Gradually he relaxed the muscles in his arms, and lowered himself down onto her gently. He kissed her mouth softly, then pressed his face into the fragrant, satiny, warm hollow between her shoulder and neck. He rested there until his heart had ceased its pounding and his breathing had slowed down.

"I don't want it to go that fast." His voice was a soft, rumbling vibration against her throat. "I want it to be good. Better than it's ever been. The best."

She cupped the back of his head and tunneled all ten fingers into the thick strands of his hair until they pressed against his scalp. "I told you that that was *never* the problem. It's always been good."

"I know. But I want this to be as special as the first time. I want us to remember this." Lovingly, adoringly, he smoothed the wayward curls off her flushed cheeks. "I love you, Brin Cassidy. I want you to know how much."

He moved far enough away from her to view her entire body. Smiling, he finished removing her panties, which were bunched around her knees. Then his eyes wandered up the entire length of her body. "You're so beautiful," he whispered.

Laying his hand first on her ankle, he let it travel

everywhere his eyes had gone, stopping to examine everything that struck his fancy.

The back of her knee . . .

"That's so soft."

"And I don't even shave there."

The light scar on her thigh . . .

"What happened here?"

"I fell onto a broken bottle at the beach."

"How old were you?"

"About six."

The mole beneath her right breast . . .

"That's beautiful."

"It's ugly."

"Not to me."

The cleft in the edge of her chin . . .

"I love this."

"I asked my mother about that once. She said before God sent me down to earth, He pointed at me and said, 'You're my favorite little angel.' That's where His finger touched me."

Riley chuckled. He took one of her hands in his and studied the patterns of veins, the dainty bone structure, the long, tapered nails. Lifting her hand to his mouth, he ardently kissed the palm, delving in its center with his tongue. She squirmed. "That tickles, but it's delicious."

"*You're* delicious."

His tongue touched the pad of her middle finger, and she reacted with a violent jerk. His eyes narrowed with the discovery. Slowly he bathed the pad of each of her fingers with that agile seducer.

"Riley," she groaned. Her back arched off the bed and her eyes fluttered closed.

They flew open when she felt her own hand being lowered to her breast. She gazed up at him with a question in her eyes. He remained silent, still, staring back at her. She wet her lips. She was suddenly shy, and terribly aroused. "You want me to . . ."

The breathless question dwindled to nothingness. He nodded. His eyes shone a brilliant blue, and his arousal was transmitted through that light. It seemed to go straight through her.

"But you never . . . said . . . never mentioned . . ."

"I think it would be beautiful to see," he said gruffly, tracing her finger where it lay against her breast. "Your fingers are still moist from my mouth."

Her feelings were ambivalent. She was timorous, yet aware of a tingling excitement deep inside her. Boldness won out over bashfulness. Loving him, wanting to please him, she began to move her hand. Then her fingers. Lightly, softly, provocatively.

A groan issued out of his throat when she had made herself ready for him. He bent down and took one sweet, ripe crest between his lips. Kissing her breasts with a mouth that seemed fashioned to give that caress, he suckled her nipples lovingly, then flicked his tongue over them repeatedly, until Brin thought she would explode from the pressure building within her.

Gauging her mounting desire, he slid his hand over her belly. His fingers sifted through the dark tuft of hair, then insinuated themselves between her quivering thighs. She closed her thighs against his hand, trapping it there, moving against it.

Tenderly he parted the velvety petals of flesh to find the wet silk they protected. He stroked her with maddening leisure. Sensitive to her needs and desires, he brought her to the brink of oblivion time and again without letting her slip over.

He kissed his way down her middle, over her tummy, her navel, her belly. His dewy lips nuzzled the V that pointed the way to the heart of her femininity. With swirling thrusts and circling strokes, his tongue expressed his unselfish love.

Modesty abandoned her. Nothing mattered except getting closer, having more, giving all. In that instant, she knew what it was to love. Her soul opened up, and all that was Brin Cassidy belonged to Jon Riley, exclusively and forever. Her spirit showered him with fragments of herself until it had all poured out. And conversely, she didn't feel empty, but full to overflowing. With love.

"Jon, no, please." She felt that her body was about to experience the release her heart had already undergone. "I want you inside me."

He let her lift him up, let her hand guide his body into the snug arbor of hers. He sank into her, deeply, as far as he could go, then reached high, higher. Trapping her head between his hands, he kissed her with all the passion pumping through him.

"Can you feel how much I love you, Brin?"

"Yes, yes, yes," she chanted in time to the driving motions of his body. "I love you, Jon. I love you."

Her climax came only seconds, heartbeats, before his. He watched her throat arch, her head toss, her face shine. Then he released his own torrent of love. It jetted into her womb and straight to her heart.

"You succeeded."

She lay draped across him. Their posture was indolent, exhausted. Idly she plucked at his chest hair. Frequently her lips puckered enough to kiss his chest.

"How's that?" he asked. His eyes were closed. He was perfectly at peace for the first time in months.

"You said you wanted us to remember this time. *I'll* never forget it."

"Forget what?"

Brin wound a clump of hair around her index finger and yanked on it hard.

"Ouch!" he exclaimed. "I'm sorry, I'm sorry. Can't you take a joke?"

Laughing, he wrapped his arms around her and rolled her to her back. He gnawed at her neck with comic enthusiasm, making the guttural sounds of a hungry jungle predator. When their lips finally made contact, the kisses they exchanged were tender and love-laden.

"I want to be your wife again, Riley," she whispered when he eventually lifted his lips from hers.

"You've never stopped being my wife."

"You're going to make me spell it out, aren't you?"

He grinned, his eyes twinkling devilishly.

"Very well." She sighed. "I want to move back into our house."

"And into our bed?"

"And into our bed." She touched his mouth. "Definitely into our bed."

"And share our lives?"

"Until we grow very old."

"What about babies?"

"What about them?"

"You didn't exactly pounce on the idea when I brought it up earlier."

"You were bleeding all over my Datsun!"

"Oh."

"Besides, we weren't officially back together then."

"It was only a matter of time."

"Don't get cocky or I won't tell you that I accidentally forgot to 'protect' myself."

"Accidentally?"

"I warned you not to get cocky."

His grin was the essence of cockiness. But he became serious when he asked, "Are you sure, Brin?"

"About the babies?"

"About it all."

There was no hesitancy in her answer. "Absolutely, positively sure."

"And what about the job with Winn? I hate asking you to give up that opportunity."

"I already have."

"You already . . . *What?* When?"

"This morning. I went downstairs and called him."

"Damn," he said softly. "Why didn't you tell me?"

"You didn't ask until now."

"What did you say to him?"

"That I was flattered by his offer, but that by accepting it, I would have to give up something far more important to me. My marriage."

"Bet he didn't take kindly to that." Riley couldn't disguise the pleasure in his voice.

"Considering that I called him before daybreak and got him out of bed, I think he took it as well as could be expected. In fact he sounded glad to hear from me so early."

"He thought you were calling to give him the good news."

"And I was," she said, snuggling against him. "It's just that my good news wasn't good news to him."

"Did you mention that you had a randy husband waiting in bed for you?"

She pecked his chin with a kiss. "Some secrets are just too delicious to share." She linked her arms around his neck. "So now are you happy? You've got your wife and your producer back."

"That sure is going to come in handy"—he kissed her—"especially if I ever get another TV show."

"Hmm, it sure—" She broke off in mid-sentence. Her head plopped back down on the pillow as she looked up at him dumbfoundedly. "What did you say?"

"I said that if I ever get another TV—"

"Okay, skip over that part and tell me what it means."

He rolled off her and lay on his back, resting his head in his left hand and propping his bandaged right one on his chest. "Dim Whit had *most* of the facts straight."

"Which ones? Is *Riley in the Morning* in trouble or not?"

"You'll be glad to know that it has gone to hell since you left it," he said, giving her an arch look. "Basically because the star of said show didn't give a damn about it anymore."

"How badly did the ratings slip?"

"Let's just say that management was justified to

call me in and issue an ultimatum. Their answer to our dilemma was to get you back. Pronto. And I was assigned the job. I was to use any means, fair or foul."

"I see."

"That's when I told them that my marriage was already in trouble and that I wasn't about to jeopardize it further for the sake of any TV show, and if that was what they expected, they could take the show and . . . I think you get my drift."

He stared at the ceiling for several moments, afraid to know her reaction. Finally he garnered his courage and turned his head. Tears were standing in her eyes. "My God, Brin, why are you crying? Are you that upset?"

She shook her head, sending crystal tears splashing over her cheeks and onto the pillow. "You did that for me?" She knew that *Riley in the Morning* meant the world to him. It was the most important thing in his life. Yet he had been willing to give it up for her. His plea for reconciliation hadn't been for the sake of his career.

"Does it bother you that you're no longer married to a star?"

"I'd love you no matter what you were."

He reached for her hand. She laid it in his left palm and he squeezed it hard. "I always knew we made a terrific team." Steeped in love, they stared at each other across the pillow.

Finally Brin found enough voice to say, "Now the crucial question. Will you make it stick?"

"What?"

"Don't play dumb with me. Your resignation. You've quit at least a dozen times that I know of and you always go back."

He laughed, then sobered. "They might not take me back this time."

"They would if they thought you were going somewhere else," she said in a sing-song voice. "They'd probably offer you a fat new contract to entice you back and guarantee that you stay."

He propped himself up on one elbow and looked down at her. "What's going on in that clever brain of yours?"

She giggled. "It stands to reason that if we get back together, make our reconciliation public knowledge and let it be known that I've been offered a spot on *Front Page*—"

"Yeah, I follow so far."

"That they'll assume you're going over to The Winn Company as host with me as producer of *Front Page*."

"But I'm not."

"They don't know that!"

"And by the time they do—"

"They'll already have begged us to come back."

"You're not only sexy, you're smart." He smacked her bare fanny with his palm and kissed her hard. They were laughing when they fell apart. "The bluff might not work, you know."

She shrugged. "Then we'll do something else. Something totally unrelated to television."

"You have that much faith in me?"

"I have that much faith in us." Her eyes became lambent, reflecting the mellow golden light of the new day. "I pulled a foolish, juvenile stunt by walking out like that, Riley. It was stupid, and I'm embarrassed about it. I've discovered what it really means to love, and I love you more than ever for forgiving me. Let's not ever let something fester between us like that again."

"Come here," he growled, hauling her close. "If we start comparing the stupid, juvenile, foolish things we've done, we'll waste precious time."

They kissed with newfound love, a love that was stronger than what they had known before. She was smiling when they drew apart. "Precious time away from what?" she asked in a sultry voice. She raised herself over him and dipped her head low on his chest, kissing and nibbling.

"Food, for one thing." Her tongue sponged his nipple, and he sucked in his breath sharply. "I never did, uh, finish that . . . that, uh . . ."

"What?"

"What?"

Her tongue was at his navel, behaving with impish impropriety. "What didn't you finish?"

"That, uh, ham sandwich. I, Brin . . . Brin?"

Her lips whispered through the thatch of dark hair above his sex. "Hmm?"

"What does a guy . . . good, merciful heaven, I'm dying . . . a guy have to, uh . . . ah, yes, like that, just like that . . . have to do to get . . . uh, break-fast?"

"I'm keeping you in bed for a good long while yet, Riley," she purred as she positioned herself above him. "I discovered a long time ago that morning is your prime time."

# THE EDITOR'S CORNER

We have four festive, touching LOVESWEPTs to complement the varied aspects of the glorious holiday season coming up.

First, remember what romance and fun you found in Joan Bramsch's **THE LIGHT SIDE** (LOVESWEPT #81)? And, especially, do you remember Sky's best friend and house mate, that magnificent model, Hooker Jablonski? Well, great news! Joan has given Hooker his very own love story ... **THE STALLION MAN**, LOVESWEPT #119. And for her modern day Romeo, Hooker, Joan has provided the perfect heroine in Juliet McLane. Juliet's a music teacher and musician ... and a "most practical lady." And it certainly isn't practical for a woman to fall for her fantasy lover! Hooker must teach the teacher a few lessons about the difference between image and reality ... and that he most definitely is flesh-and-blood reality! You'll relish this warm romance from talented Joan Bramsch.

How many times I've told you in our Editor's Corner about our great pleasure in finding and presenting a brand new romance writer. That is such a genuine sentiment shared by all of us at LOVESWEPT. So it is with much delight that we publish next month Hertha Schulze's first love story, **BEFORE AND AFTER**, LOVESWEPT #120. And what a debut book this is! Heroine Libby Carstairs is a little pudgy, a little dowdy, and a heck of a brainy Ph.D. student. Hero Blake Faulkner is a very worldly, very successful fashion photographer, and one heck of a man! He makes a reckless wager with a pompous make-up artist that he can turn Libby into a cover girl in just a few short weeks. Mildly insulted, but intrigued, Libby goes along with the bet ... then she begins to fall for the devastating Blake and the gambol turns serious. We think you're going to adore this thoroughly charming and chuckle-filled Pygmalion-type romance! And what a nifty, heartwarming twist it takes at the end!

**TEMPEST**, LOVESWEPT #121, marks the return to our list of the much loved Helen Mittermeyer. With her characteristic verve and storytelling force Helen gives us

*(continued)*

the passionate love story of Sage and Ross Tempest, whose love affair throughout their marriage has been stormy (which may even be putting it mildly). And, as always, you can count on Helen to enhance her romance with the endearing elements, as well as the downright funny ones that make her such a popular author. You'll long remember little Pip and Tad, not just Sage and Ross . . . and one very special, very naughty turkey!

**A SUMMER SMILE**, LOVESWEPT #122, by Iris Johansen is guaranteed to warm your heart and soul no matter how blustery the day is next month when you read it. Iris brings together two of her wonderfully memorable characters for their own bold, exciting love story. Daniel Seifert—remember Beau's captain in **BLUE VELVET**?— is given a hair-raising assignment to rescue a young woman from terrorists. She is Zilah, whom David took under his wing (**TOUCH THE HORIZON**) and helped to heal. Sparks fly—literally and figuratively—between this unlikely couple as they flee through the desert to safety in Sedikhan. Yet, learning Zilah's tragic secret, Daniel is frozen with fear . . . fear that only **A SUMMER SMILE** can melt. Oh, what a romantic reading experience this is!

All of us at LOVESWEPT wish you the happiest of holiday seasons.

Sincerely,

*Carolyn Nichols*

Carolyn Nichols
  Editor
*LOVESWEPT*
Bantam Books, Inc.
666 Fifth Avenue
New York, NY 10103


P.S. In case you forgot to send in your questionnaire last month, we're running it again on the next page. We'd really appreciate it if you could take the time and trouble to fill it out and return it to us.

Dear Reader:

As you know, our goal is to give you a "keeper" with every love story we publish. In our view a "keeper" blends the traditional beloved elements of a romance with truly original ingredients of characterization or plot or setting. Breaking new ground can be risky, but it's well worth it when one succeeds. We hope we succeed almost all the time. Now, well on the road to our third anniversary, we would appreciate a progress report from you. Please take a moment to let us know how you think we're doing.

1. Overall the quality of our stories has *improved* ☐
   *declined* ☐
   *remained the same* ☐

2. Would you trust us to increase the number of books we publish each month without sacrificing quality?   *yes* ☐   *no* ☐

3. How many romances do you buy each month? _____

4. Which romance brands do you regularly read?

   _____

   _____

   _____

   _____

   _____

   _____

   *I choose my books by author, not brand name* ☐

5. Please list your three favorite authors from other lines:

6. Please list your six favorite LOVESWEPT authors:

7. Would you be interested in buying reprinted editions of your favorite LOVESWEPT authors' romances published in the early months of the line?

8. Is there a special message you have for us? (Attach a page, if necessary.)

   With our thanks to you for taking the time and trouble to respond,

Sincerely,

*Carolyn Nichols*

Carolyn Nichols—for everyone at LOVESWEPT

Valentina—she's a beauty, an enigma, a warm,
sensitive woman, a screen idol . . . goddess.

# GODDESS

## By Margaret Pemberton

There was a sound of laughter, of glasses clink-
ing. A sense of excitement so deep it nearly
took her breath away, seized her. With glowing
eyes Valentina stepped into the noise and heat
of the party.

"Lilli wants to meet you," a girl with a
friendly smile said, grabbing hold of Valentina's
hand and tugging her into the throng. "I'm
Patsy Smythe. Have you met Lilli before?"

"No," Daisy said, avoiding the apprecia-
tive touch of a strange male hand.

Patsy grinned. "Just treat her as if she's the
Queen of Sheba and you won't go far wrong.

Oh, someone has spilled rum on my skirt. How do you get rum stains out of chiffon?''

Valentina didn't know. Her gaze met Lilli Rainer's. Lilli's eyes were small and piercing, raisin-black in a powdered white face. She had been talking volubly, a long jade cigarette holder stabbing the air to emphasize her remarks. Now she halted, her anecdote forgotten. She had lived and breathed for the camera. Only talkies had defeated her. Her voice held the guttural tones of her native Germany and no amount of elocution lessons had been able to eradicate them. She had retired gracefully, allowing nobody to know of her bitter frustration. On seeing Valentina, she rose imperiously to her feet. No star or starlet from Worldwide Studios had been invited to the party. She did not like to be outshone and the girl before her, with her effortless grace and dark, fathom-deep eyes was doing just that. Everyone had turned in her direction as Patsy Smythe had led her across the room.

Lilli's carmine-painted lips tightened. "This is not a studio party," she said icily. "Admittance is by invitation only."

Valentina smiled. "I've been invited," she said pleasantly. "I came with Bob Kelly."

Lilli sat down slowly and gestured away those surrounding them. The amethyst satin dress Valentina wore was pathetically cheap and yet it looked marvelous on the girl. A spasm of jealousy caught at her aged throat and was gone. It was only the second rate that she could not tolerate. And the girl in front of her was far from second rate. "Do you work at Worldwide?" she asked sharply.

"No."

"Then you ought to," Lilli said tersely, "It's a first-rate studio and it has one of the best directors in town." She drew on her cigarette, inhaling deeply. "Where is Bob going to take you? Warner Brothers? Universal?"

"Not to any one of them," Valentina said composedly, not allowing her inner emotions to show. "Bob doesn't want me to work at the studios."

Lilli blew a wreath of smoke into the air and stared at her. "Then he's a fool," she said tartly. "You belong in front of the cameras. Anyone with half an eye can see that."

Noise rose and ebbed about them. Neither of them heard it.

"I know," Valentina said sharply and with breathtaking candor. "But Bob doesn't. Not yet."

Lilli crushed her cigarette out viciously. "And how long are you going to wait until he wakes up to reality? Whose life are you leading? Yours or his?" She leaned forward, grasping hold of Valentina's wrist, her eyes brilliant.

"There are very few, my child, a very tiny few, who can be instantly beloved by the cameras. It's nothing that can be learned. It's something you are born with. It's in here . . ." She stabbed at her head with a lacquered fingernail, "and in here . . ." She slapped her hand across her corseted stomach. "It's *inside* you. It's not actions and gestures, it's something that is innate." She released Valentina's wrist and leaned back in her chair. "And you have it."

Valentina could feel her heart beating in short, sharp strokes. Lilli was telling her what she already knew, and it was almost more than she could bear.

She had to get away. She needed peace and quiet in order to be able to think clearly. To still the unsettling emotions Lilli's words had aroused.

She fought her way from the crowded room into the ornate entrance hall. A chandelier hung brilliantly above her head; the carpet was wine-red, the walls covered in silk. There was a marble telephone stand and a dark, carved wooden chair beside it. She sat down, her legs trembling as if she were on the edge of an abyss. Someone had left cigarettes and a lighter on the telephone table. Clumsily she spilled them from their pack, picking one up, struggling with the lighter.

"Allow me," a deep-timbred voice said from the shadows of the stairs. The lighter clattered to the table, the cigarette dropped from her fingers as she whirled her head round.

He had been sitting on the stairs, just out of range of the chandelier's brilliance. Now he moved, rising to his feet, walking toward her with the athletic ease and sexual negligence of a natural born predator.

She couldn't speak, couldn't move. He withdrew a black Sobrainie from a gold cigarette case, lit it, inhaling deeply and then removed the cigarette from his mouth and set it gently between her lips.

She was shaking. Over the abyss and falling. Falling as Vidal Rakoczi softly murmured her name.

## Goddess

* * *

There was still noise. Laughter and music were still loud in nearby rooms but Valentina was oblivious to it. She was aware of nothing but the dark, magnetic face staring down at her, the eyes pinning her in place, consuming her like dry tinder in a forest fire. She tried to stand, to gather some semblance of dignity, but could do neither. The wine-red of the walls and carpet, the brilliance of the chandelier, all spun around her in a dizzy vortex of light and color and in the center, drawing her like a moth to a flame, were the burning eyes of Vidal Rakoczi. She was suffocating, unable to breathe, to draw air into her lungs. The cigarette fell from her lips, scorching the amethyst satin. Swiftly he swept it from her knees, crushing it beneath his foot.

"Are you hurt?" The depth of feeling in his voice shocked her into mobility.

"I . . . No . . ." Unsteadily she rose to her feet. He made no movement to stand aside, to allow her to pass.

He was so close that she could feel the warmth of his breath on her cheek, smell the indefinable aroma of his maleness.

"Will you excuse me?" she asked, a pulse beating wildly in her throat.

"No." The gravity in his voice held her transfixed. His eyes had narrowed. They were bold and black and blatantly determined. "Now that I have found you again, I shall never excuse you to leave me. Not ever."

## Goddess

She felt herself sway and his hand grasped her arm, steadying her.

"Let's go where we can talk."

"No," she whispered, suddenly terrified as her dreams took on reality. She tried to pull away from him but he held her easily.

"Why not?" A black brow rose questioningly.

The touch of his hand seared her flesh. She could not go with him. To go with him would be to abandon Bob and that was unthinkable. He had done nothing to deserve such disloyalty. He had been kind to her. Kinder than anyone else had ever been. Sobs choked her throat. She loved Bob, but not in the way that he needed her to love him. The day would have come when she would have had to tell him so . . . but it hadn't come, and she couldn't just leave with Rakoczi. Not like this.

"No," she said again, her lips dry, her mouth parched. "Please let me go."

The strong, olive-toned hand tightened on her arm and the earth seemed to tremble beneath her feet. It was as if the very foundations upon which she had built her life since leaving the convent were cracking and crumbling around her. She made one last, valiant attempt to cling to the world that had been her haven.

"I came with Bob Kelly," she said, knowing even as she spoke that her battle was lost. "He will be looking for me."

A slight smile curved the corners of his mouth. "But he won't find you," he said. With devastating assurance he took her hand, and the course of her life changed.

# Goddess

She wasn't aware of leaving the house. She wasn't aware of anything but Vidal Rakoczi's hand tightly imprisoning hers as she ran to keep up with his swift stride.

She sat in silence at his side in his car, peace and contentment lost to her forever. Something long dormant had at last been released. A zest, a recklessness for life that caused the blood to pound along her veins, and her nerve ends to throb. Like had met like. She had known it instinctively the day he had stalked across to her on the studio lot. Now there was no going back. No acceptance of anything less than life with the man who was at her side.

The car crowned a dune and he braked and halted. In the moonlight the heaving Pacific was silk-black, the swelling waves breaking into surging foam on a crescent of firm white sand. The night breeze from the sea was salt-laden and chilly. He took off his dinner jacket and draped it around her shoulders as they slipped and slid down the dunes to the beach. She stepped out of her high-heeled sandals, raising her face to the breeze.

"It's very beautiful here. And very lonely."

"That's why I come."

They walked down along in silence for a while, the Pacific breakers creaming and running up the shoreline only inches from their feet.

"You know what it is I want of you, don't you?" he asked at last, and a shiver ran down her spine. Whatever it was, she would give it freely. "I want to film you. To see if the luminous quality you posess transfers to the screen."

## Goddess

The moon slid out from behind a bank of clouds. He had expected lavish thanks; vows of eternal gratitude; a silly stream of nonsense about how she had always wanted to be a movie star. Instead she remained silent, her face strangely serene. There was an inner stillness to her that he found profoundly refreshing. He picked up a pebble and skimmed it far out into the night-black sea.

"I am a man of instincts," he said, stating a fact that no one who had come into contact with him would deny. "I believe that you have a rare gift, Valentina." Their hands touched fleetingly and she trembled. "I expect complete obedience. Absolute discipline."

His brows were pulled close together, his silhouetted face that of a Roman emperor accustomed to wielding total power. He halted, staring down at her. "Do you understand?"

Her head barely reached his shoulder. She turned her face up to his, the sea-breeze fanning her hair softly against her cheeks. The moonlight accentuated the breath-taking purity of her cheekbone and jaw line.

"Yes," she said, and at her composure his eyes gleamed with amusement.

"Where the devil did you spring from?" he asked, a smile touching his mouth.

Her eyes sparkled in the darkness as she said with steely determination. "Wherever it was, I'm not going back."

He began to laugh and as he did so she stumbled, falling against him. His arms closed around her, steadying her. For a second they remained motionless and then the laughter faded from his eyes and he lowered his head, his mouth claiming hers in swift, sure contact.

Nothing had prepared her for Vidal's kiss. Her lips trembled and then parted willingly beneath his. There was sudden shock and an onrush of pleasure as his tongue sought and demanded hers, setting her on fire.

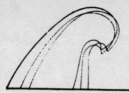 **LOVESWEPT**

## Love Stories you'll never forget
## by authors you'll always remember

| | | |
|---|---|---|
| ☐ 21603 | **Heaven's Price** #1 Sandra Brown | $1.95 |
| ☐ 21604 | **Surrender** #2 Helen Mittermeyer | $1.95 |
| ☐ 21600 | **The Joining Stone** #3 Noelle Berry McCue | $1.95 |
| ☐ 21601 | **Silver Miracles** #4 Fayrene Preston | $1.95 |
| ☐ 21605 | **Matching Wits** #5 Carla Neggers | $1.95 |
| ☐ 21606 | **A Love for All Time** #6 Dorothy Garlock | $1.95 |
| ☐ 21609 | **Hard Drivin' Man** #10 Nancy Carlson | $1.95 |
| ☐ 21611 | **Hunter's Payne** #12 Joan J. Domning | $1.95 |
| ☐ 21618 | **Tiger Lady** #13 Joan Domning | $1.95 |
| ☐ 21614 | **Brief Delight** #15 Helen Mittermeyer | $1.95 |
| ☐ 21639 | **The Planting Season** #33 Dorothy Garlock | $1.95 |
| ☐ 21627 | **The Trustworthy Redhead** #35 Iris Johansen | $1.95 |

<u>**Prices and availability subject to change without notice.**</u>

**Buy them at your local bookstore or use this handy coupon for ordering:**

---

**Bantam Books, Inc., Dept. SW, 414 East Golf Road, Des Plaines, Ill. 60016**

Please send me the books I have checked above. I am enclosing $_____
(please add $1.25 to cover postage and handling). Send check or money order
—no cash or C.O.D.'s please.

Mr/Mrs/Miss_____

Address_____

City_____State/Zip_____

SW—10/85

Please allow four to six weeks for delivery. This offer expires 4/86.

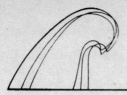

# LOVESWEPT

## *Love Stories you'll never forget by authors you'll always remember*

| | | | |
|---|---|---|---|
| ☐ | 21709 | **Fascination #99** Joan Elliott Pickart | $2.25 |
| ☐ | 21710 | **The Goodies Case #100** Sara Orwig | $2.25 |
| ☐ | 21711 | **Worthy Opponents #101** Marianne Shock | $2.25 |
| ☐ | 21713 | **Remember Me, Love? #102** Eugenia Riley | $2.25 |
| ☐ | 21708 | **Out of This World #103** Nancy Holder | $2.25 |
| ☐ | 21674 | **Suspicion #104** Millie Grey | $2.25 |
| ☐ | 21714 | **The Shadowless Day #105** Joan Elliot Pickart | $2.25 |
| ☐ | 21715 | **Taming Maggie #106** Peggy Web | $2.25 |
| ☐ | 21699 | **Rachel's Confession #107** Fayrene Preston | $2.25 |
| ☐ | 21716 | **A Tough Act to Follow #108** Billie Green | $2.25 |
| ☐ | 21718 | **Come As You Are #109** Laurien Berenson | $2.25 |
| ☐ | 21719 | **Sunlight's Promise #110** Joan Elliott Pickart | $2.25 |
| ☐ | 21726 | **Dear Mitt #111** Sara Orwig | $2.25 |
| ☐ | 21729 | **Birds Of A Feather #112** Peggy Web | $2.25 |
| ☐ | 21727 | **A Matter of Magic #113** Linda Hampton | $2.25 |
| ☐ | 21728 | **Rainbow's Angel #114** Joan Elliott Pickart | $2.25 |

### Prices and availability subject to change without notice.

**Buy them at your local bookstore or use this handy coupon for ordering:**

---

Bantam Books, Inc., Dept. SW2, 414 East Golf Road, Des Plaines, Ill. 60016

Please send me the books I have checked above. I am enclosing $_____
(please add $1.25 to cover postage and handling). Send check or money order
—no cash or C.O.D.'s please.

Mr/Mrs/Miss_____

Address_____

City_____State/Zip_____

SW2—10/85

Please allow four to six weeks for delivery. This offer expires 4/86.

# LOVESWEPT

*Love Stories you'll never forget
by authors you'll always remember*

# LOVESWEPT

## *Love Stories you'll never forget by authors you'll always remember*